Also by Rachael Reed

Codefendant
Codefendant
Once a Cheater
Once a Cheater
Passport Bro
What Happens in Prison
Preference
Sprinkle Sprinkle
Championship Bad
Street Exodus
Street Exodus
Street Royalty
Pawns of Power
SIS
Cartel Bloodline
Get Money Girls
Skip the Games
Til Death Do Us Part
Backpage Hustle
Link in Bio
The Virgin and The Kingpin
A Gangsta's Heart
Boosters
Can't Turn a Hoe Into a Housewife

Can't Turn a Hoe Into a Housewife

Rachael Reed
©2024

Check Out More Great Products and Free Giveaways
https://tbdbpublishing.com/

Chapter 1: Life on the Streets

Erica sat on the plush leather couch in her upscale apartment, the city lights flickering through the window like distant stars. She wore a sleek, form-fitting dress that clung to her curves, her makeup flawless, her hair cascading in perfect waves. On the surface, she looked like she had it all—money, beauty, power. But beneath the glamorous exterior was a woman trapped in a life she desperately wanted to escape.

The night was still young, but Erica felt the weight of exhaustion pressing down on her. It wasn't just the physical fatigue; it was the emotional toll of living a double life. She was a seasoned escort, one of Lil Ron's top earners. She knew the game inside and out, how to play her clients, how to keep them coming back for more. But the excitement that once thrilled her had faded, replaced by a gnawing emptiness that grew with each passing day.

Lil Ron had discovered her five years ago, a fresh face with a hunger for the fast life. He'd promised her the world, and in a way, he delivered. He set her up in a nice place, gave her access to the city's elite, and made sure she was always in the finest clothes and jewelry. But there was a price to pay, and Erica was paying it every day. Lil Ron controlled everything—her money, her schedule, even her freedom. He was charming when he needed to be, but his charm was a thin veneer over a dangerous temper. Erica had seen it firsthand, the way he dealt with girls who stepped out of line. She knew better than to cross him.

The apartment door opened, and Lil Ron strolled in, a smirk on his face. He was dressed in his usual flashy style, all designer brands and gold chains. He carried an air of confidence, a man who knew he was untouchable. He tossed a thick envelope onto the coffee table, the sound of cash rustling inside.

"That's your cut," he said, his voice smooth and low. "Did good last night. Clients loved you."

Erica forced a smile, picking up the envelope. The money was good, better than most could dream of. But it felt dirty, tainted by the life she led. She glanced at Lil Ron, trying to read his mood. He could be unpredictable, and she needed to stay on his good side.

"Thanks, Ron," she said, her voice steady. "Just doing my job."

Lil Ron chuckled, a dark glint in his eyes. "Yeah, well, you keepin' me happy, keepin' the clients happy. That's all that matters."

Erica nodded, her stomach twisting. She hated how she had to play along, how she had to pretend everything was fine. She looked around the apartment, at the expensive furniture, the designer clothes in her closet. It all felt so empty, so meaningless. She wanted more, something real. But in this world, "real" was a luxury she couldn't afford.

As Lil Ron made himself comfortable, Erica excused herself to the bathroom. She needed a moment to herself, to breathe. She looked in the mirror, her reflection staring back at her. The makeup, the clothes, the jewelry—it was all a mask, hiding the woman beneath. She felt a pang of longing for a normal life, a life where she didn't have to sell herself to survive. She thought about the girls she saw on the streets, the ones who didn't have the "luxury" she had. They were out there hustling, doing whatever it took to make ends meet. She wasn't any different, just had a better facade.

Erica turned on the faucet, splashing cold water on her face. She felt a tear slip down her cheek and quickly wiped it away. Crying wouldn't solve anything. She had to stay strong, had to keep her head in the game. But deep down, she knew she was reaching her breaking point. The life she was living wasn't sustainable. It was dangerous, filled with pitfalls and traps. She'd seen too many girls fall, and she didn't want to be next.

As she dried her face, her phone buzzed with a new message. It was from one of her regulars, a wealthy businessman who paid top dollar for her time. He wanted to see her tonight, offering more money than usual. Erica felt a surge of nausea. She didn't want to go, didn't want to put on the act again. But she had no choice. This was her life, her reality.

She stepped out of the bathroom, her mask firmly back in place. Lil Ron glanced up at her, his eyes cold and calculating. "You got a gig tonight," he said, more of a statement than a question. "Don't keep him waiting."

Erica nodded, grabbing her purse. She headed for the door, feeling like a prisoner walking to her cell. She knew what she was, what she had to do. But she couldn't help but dream of something better. As she stepped into the hallway, she paused, looking back at the apartment. The luxurious trappings felt like a cage, trapping her in a life she didn't want.

She took a deep breath and stepped into the elevator. As the doors closed, she felt the weight of her choices pressing down on her. She had to find a way out, had to break free from the chains that bound her. But in this world, breaking free came with a price. And Erica wasn't sure if she was ready to pay it.

As the elevator descended, Erica felt a growing sense of determination. She needed to escape this life, to find something real. But she knew it wouldn't be easy. Lil Ron wasn't going to let her go without a fight. She had to be smart, had to plan her escape carefully. She thought about the other girls, the ones who had tried to leave. They were either fucked up, missing, or worse. But Erica was different. She had a chance, a slim one, but a chance nonetheless.

She stepped out of the elevator and into the bustling streets. The city was alive with energy, a cacophony of sounds and sights. Erica walked down the sidewalk, blending into the crowd. She felt a thrill of anonymity, a momentary escape from the life she knew. But it was fleeting. Her phone buzzed again, a reminder of the life she couldn't escape.

Erica took a deep breath, steeling herself for the night ahead. She knew she had to keep up the facade, to play the role she'd been playing for so long. But she also knew that something had to change. She couldn't keep living this double life, trapped between the woman she was and the woman she wanted to be.

As she hailed a cab and climbed inside, Erica made a silent promise to herself. She would find a way out, find a way to escape the life that had ensnared her. But for now, she had to survive. The streets were unforgiving, and in this world, only the strong survived. Erica knew she had to be strong, to play the game until she could find a way out. And when that day came, she would finally be free.

The cab pulled away from the curb, merging into the city's flow. Erica stared out the window, her thoughts a whirlwind of plans and possibilities. She knew it wouldn't be easy, but she was ready to fight for her freedom. The life she was living was dangerous, filled with shadows and secrets. But Erica was determined to find the light, to break free from the darkness that threatened to consume her.

As the city lights blurred into a kaleidoscope of colors, Erica felt a glimmer of hope. The streets had shaped her, molded her into the woman she was. But they wouldn't define her. Erica was ready to take control, to carve out a new path for herself. She was ready to leave that life behind. But for tonight it's business as usual.

Chapter 2: A Chance Encounter

The night was alive with the bass-heavy beats of hip-hop, the air thick with the scent of weed and sweat. The party was in full swing, packed with people grinding and swaying to the music. It was one of those exclusive spots, a place where the city's elite mixed with the street's finest. Erica moved through the crowd like a seasoned pro, her curves wrapped in a tight, red dress that left little to the imagination. She was there to work, but her mind was somewhere else, lost in the murky waters of her thoughts.

Lil Ron had sent her to this party to network, to scope out potential clients. He called it "expanding the business," but Erica knew it was just another night of the same old shit. The crowd was a mix of hustlers, ballers, and high-rolling wannabes, all looking to flaunt their wealth and status. Erica had been to a hundred parties like this, and they all felt the same—empty and fake. But tonight, something felt different. There was an energy in the air, a sense of something unexpected.

Erica found herself at the bar, nursing a drink and scanning the room. Her eyes landed on a tall, broad-shouldered man standing across the room. He was dressed casually, a crisp white shirt, and dark jeans, looking out of place among the flashy crowd. There was something about him, a quiet confidence that drew her in. He wasn't like the others, flaunting their wealth and status. He seemed real, grounded.

She watched him for a while, curious. He caught her eye and smiled, a genuine smile that reached his eyes. Erica felt a flutter in her chest, a feeling she hadn't felt in a long time. She looked away, trying to play it cool, but she felt his gaze on her. A moment later, he was walking over, cutting through the crowd with ease.

"Hey," he said, his voice deep and smooth. "You look like you could use some company."

Erica raised an eyebrow, a smirk playing on her lips. "You think you can keep up?"

He chuckled, leaning against the bar. "I can try. I'm Quan."

"Erica," she replied, extending her hand. He took it, his grip firm and warm. There was a spark between them, an electric connection that sent a shiver down her spine. They made small talk, the conversation flowing easily. Quan had a way of making her feel at ease, like she could be herself without putting on a show. It was refreshing, a stark contrast to the men she usually dealt with.

As they talked, Erica found herself opening up, laughing at his jokes and sharing stories about her life. She felt a strange sense of comfort with him, a feeling she hadn't experienced in a long time. Quan was different. He was respectful, genuine, and treated her like a person, not a commodity. It was a stark contrast to the men who usually came into her life, looking for a good time and nothing more.

They spent the rest of the night together, dancing and talking. Erica felt herself letting go, enjoying the moment. She hadn't felt this alive in years. Quan was charming, but in a way that felt sincere. He wasn't trying to impress her with money or status; he was just being himself. And Erica found herself drawn to him, intrigued by the man behind the cool exterior.

As the night wore on, the party started to wind down. People began to leave, but Erica and Quan stayed, caught up in their conversation. They ended up on the rooftop, overlooking the city. The view was breathtaking, the lights of the city stretching out below them. Erica leaned against the railing, looking out at the skyline. Quan stood beside her, his presence comforting.

"This city's crazy, ain't it?" he said, his voice soft.

Erica nodded, her eyes fixed on the horizon. "Yeah, it is. But it's home."

Quan turned to her, his gaze intense. "You ever think about leaving? Starting over somewhere else?"

Erica felt a pang in her chest. She had thought about it, dreamed about it. But the reality was, she was trapped. Trapped by Lil Ron, by her past, by her own choices. She sighed, shaking her head. "Yeah, but it's not that easy."

Quan nodded, his eyes understanding. "I get that. But sometimes, you gotta take a leap. You never know where you might land."

Erica looked at him, her heart racing. There was something about the way he looked at her, like he could see right through her. She felt exposed, vulnerable, but in a way that made her feel alive. She bit her lip, hesitating. She didn't want to get her hopes up, but she couldn't deny the pull she felt towards him.

Quan reached into his pocket, pulling out his phone. "Here, give me your number. Maybe we can hang out sometime. No pressure, just... friends."

Erica felt a rush of excitement. She took his phone, quickly typing in her number. It was a small gesture, but it felt like a step towards something new, something different. She handed the phone back, their fingers brushing. There was a spark, a connection that neither of them could deny.

"Thanks," Erica said, her voice soft. "For tonight. I needed this."

Quan smiled, his eyes warm. "Me too. It was nice to meet someone real for a change."

Erica felt a warmth spread through her chest. She had spent so long building walls, keeping people at a distance. But with Quan, it felt different. She felt seen, understood. It was scary, but also exhilarating. She knew she had to be careful, but for the first time in a long time, she felt a glimmer of hope.

As they walked back inside, Erica felt a sense of lightness. She had no idea where things would go with Quan, but she was willing to find out. It was a risk, but it was one she was willing to take. She felt a thrill of excitement, a feeling she hadn't experienced in years.

They exchanged a lingering goodbye, and Erica watched as Quan walked away, disappearing into the night. She stood there for a moment, feeling a strange mix of emotions. She knew she was playing with fire, but she couldn't help herself. There was something about Quan that drew her in, made her want to take a chance.

As she made her way back to her apartment, Erica couldn't stop thinking about Quan. His smile, his voice, the way he made her feel. It was weird, getting involved with someone like him. But she couldn't deny the attraction, the connection. She felt a thrill of excitement, a sense of possibility. Maybe, just maybe, this was the beginning of something new.

Erica entered her apartment, the door clicking shut behind her. She leaned against it, her mind racing. She knew she had to be careful, that she couldn't let her guard down. But for the first time in a long time, she felt a spark of hope. The life she knew was dangerous, filled with shadows and secrets. But with Quan, she felt a glimmer of light, a chance for something real.

As she got ready for bed, Erica felt a sense of excitement and anticipation. She didn't know what the future held, but she was ready to find out. The night had been unexpected, a chance encounter that had turned her world upside down. She felt a thrill of uncertainty, a sense of adventure. It was a dangerous game, but Erica was ready to play. The streets had taught her to be tough, to survive. But now, she was ready to live. She was ready to take a chance on something real.

As Erica lay in bed, her mind replaying the night's events, she felt a sense of calm. She had no idea what would happen next, but she was ready for whatever came her way. She was ready to take control, to carve out a new path for herself. She felt like anything was possible.

Chapter 3: The Beginning of Something New

Quan's apartment was small but cozy, tucked away in a quiet neighborhood far from the chaos of the streets. It was a stark contrast to the lavish yet hollow life Erica knew. The walls were lined with bookshelves filled with old novels and history books, a worn-out couch sat in the center, and the faint aroma of coffee lingered in the air. It felt real, lived-in, a place where someone had carved out a space of peace amidst the storm.

Quan himself was a mystery to most. Born and raised in the heart of the city, he had seen his fair share of hardships. He grew up with a single mother, hustling to make ends meet while his father served time. The streets had tried to pull him in, but Quan had resisted, determined to build a life that wasn't defined by crime and chaos. He worked a steady job at a community center, mentoring kids and keeping them off the streets. It wasn't glamorous, but it was honest, and it gave him purpose.

As Quan and Erica spent more time together, she saw the depth of his character. He was genuine, kind-hearted, and grounded, qualities that stood out in a world filled with fake personas and ulterior motives. They started dating, their connection deepening with each encounter. Quan treated her differently—he wasn't interested in her body, her money, or the image she portrayed. He saw her for who she was, flaws and all, and that scared Erica more than anything. It was real, and real was something she wasn't used to.

They would go on simple dates, walking through the park, grabbing a bite at a local diner, or just chilling at his place. Quan would tell her about his work, the kids he mentored, and the struggles they faced. Erica would listen, captivated by his passion and dedication. He was trying to make a difference, to break the cycle of poverty and crime that ensnared so many. It was a stark contrast to her life, where survival meant doing whatever it took, no matter the cost.

One night, they sat on his couch, the room dimly lit by the soft glow of a lamp. Quan had cooked dinner, a simple meal of pasta and salad. They talked about everything and nothing, the conversation flowing easily. Erica felt a warmth in her chest, a feeling of comfort she hadn't experienced in years. She found herself opening up to him, sharing stories from her past, her dreams, her fears. It was scary, letting her guard down, but with Quan, it felt safe.

"You ever think 'bout leavin' the city?" Quan asked, his voice soft.

Erica looked down, her fingers tracing patterns on the couch. "Yeah, sometimes. But it's hard, y'know?

Quan nodded, his eyes filled with understanding. "I get that. But you gotta think about what's easy, Erica. Sometimes we can make things too complicated. You deserve a real shot at happiness."

Erica felt a lump form in her throat. It was the first time someone had said that to her, genuinely meant it. She blinked back tears, trying to keep her composure. "I don't know if I even know what happiness looks like anymore."

Quan reached out, gently cupping her cheek. "It's whatever you want it to be. And you can have it, but you gotta believe that. You gotta believe you worth it."

His words hit her hard, breaking down the walls she had built around herself. She leaned into his touch, feeling a tear slip down her cheek. It was terrifying, the thought of opening herself up to the possibility of something real, something good. But it was also exhilarating. Quan made her feel things she hadn't felt in a long time—hope, desire, a yearning for something more.

Their relationship blossomed, each day bringing them closer. They would talk for hours, about their lives, their hopes, their dreams. Erica found herself thinking about a future with Quan, a future away from the streets, away from Lil Ron. It was a dangerous thought, but it was also intoxicating. She started to see a way out, a path to a life she had never dared to dream of.

But reality was never far away. Erica knew the risks, knew that Lil Ron wouldn't let her go easily. He had a hold on her, a grip she couldn't shake. She was one of his best earners, and he wouldn't let her walk away without a fight. The thought of confronting him, of telling him she wanted out, filled her with dread. But she felt stronger, more determined. She knew she had to make a choice, to take a leap of faith.

One night, after a long day at work, Quan invited Erica over. He had something to show her. She arrived, curious and excited. Quan led her to a small room at the back of his apartment. The room was bare, except for a canvas on an easel and a table filled with art supplies.

"I been workin' on somethin'," Quan said, a shy smile on his face. "It's kinda personal, but I wanna share it with you."

Erica felt a thrill of anticipation. She watched as Quan uncovered the canvas, revealing a beautiful painting. It was a portrait of a woman, her eyes filled with strength and vulnerability. It took Erica a moment to realize it was her.

"Quan... this is..." Erica was at a loss for words, her eyes welling up with tears.

Quan stepped closer, his eyes never leaving hers. "I wanted to capture you, the real you. Not the persona you put on for the world, but the person I see. The person I care about."

Erica felt her heart swell with emotion. She had never felt so seen, so understood. She reached out, her fingers grazing the canvas. "It's beautiful, Quan. I... I don't know what to say."

Quan smiled, his eyes soft and warm. "You don't gotta say nothin'. Just... know that I'm here for you. Whatever you need."

Erica looked at him, her heart racing. She felt a surge of emotion, a mix of fear and excitement. She knew she was falling for him, hard and fast. It was dangerous, but she couldn't help herself. Quan was everything she had ever wanted, everything she had ever needed.

She stepped closer, her breath hitching. Quan reached out, pulling her into a gentle kiss. It was soft, tender, filled with unspoken promises. Erica melted into him, her arms wrapping around his neck. It was a moment of pure connection, a glimpse of the future she so desperately craved.

As they pulled away, Erica felt a warmth spread through her chest. She knew she had to make a choice, to take a leap of faith. The life she had known was dangerous, filled with darkness and deceit. But with Quan, she saw a glimmer of light, a chance for something real.

As they sat together, wrapped in each other's arms, Erica felt a sense of peace. It was a new beginning, a chance to start over. She knew it wouldn't be easy, that there would be obstacles and challenges ahead. But she was ready to face them, to fight for the life she wanted.

Deep down, she knew the road ahead would be treacherous. Lil Ron was a dangerous man, and he wouldn't let her go without a fight. Erica felt a chill run down her spine, the reality of her situation settling in. She had to be smart, had to plan her escape carefully. But for now, she allowed herself to bask in the warmth of Quan's love, the promise of a brighter future.

As the night wore on, Erica and Quan lay together, their bodies entwined. They talked about their dreams, their hopes for the future. It was a moment of pure bliss, a glimpse of the life they could have. Erica knew she had to fight for it, to break free from the chains that bound her.

The beginning of something new, something real. Erica was ready to leave the darkness behind and step into the light. The stakes were high, but the reward was worth it. Erica knew she had to be brave, to take a leap of faith. And with Quan, she was ready to do just that. The future was uncertain, but for the first time in a long time, Erica felt hopeful. She was ready to fight for her happiness, for the life she deserved. And nothing, not even Lil Ron, would stand in her way.

Chapter 4: The Double Life Struggle

Erica's world had always been divided. By day, she was a woman wrapped in silk and diamonds, an escort catering to the city's elite. By night, she was with Quan, a man who saw past her facade and into her heart. Balancing these two lives was a constant struggle, and the lines between them were beginning to blur. As her feelings for Quan grew, her commitment to her work waned., and she knew it. But the allure of a normal life, a life with Quan, was too tempting to resist.

Lil Ron had a nose for trouble. He could sense when one of his girls was slipping, losing their edge. And Erica was slipping. She was still bringing in the money, but her enthusiasm had dulled. She wasn't as sharp, not as focused. Ron had noticed the change, and it worried him. Erica was one of his best money makers, and he couldn't afford to lose her or the money.

Erica sat in her apartment, staring at her reflection in the mirror. She was getting ready for another night out, another client. Her makeup was flawless, her dress clung to her curves, but she felt empty inside. She thought about Quan, about the life they could have together. It was a dream she clung to, a beacon of hope in the darkness. But every time she looked in the mirror, she was reminded of the reality she couldn't escape. She was trapped, caught between two worlds.

The doorbell rang, snapping her out of her thoughts. She quickly composed herself, slipping into the role she knew so well. The client was a regular, a wealthy businessman with a penchant for control. Erica knew how to play the game, how to be what he wanted. But tonight, her heart wasn't in it. Her mind was elsewhere, with Quan.

After the client left, Erica felt a wave of disgust wash over her. She quickly showered, scrubbing away the remnants of the night. She wanted to wash away the guilt, the shame, but it clung to her like a second skin. She sat on the edge of her bed, her phone in her hand. She wanted to call Quan, to hear his voice, but she hesitated. She didn't want to drag him into her world, a world filled with darkness and danger.

Meanwhile, Lil Ron was busy with his own business. He had a network of informants, people who kept him in the loop. He heard whispers about Erica, about her slacking off. It didn't sit right with him. Erica had always been reliable, always on point. But now, something was different. He couldn't shake the feeling that she was hiding something. He decided to keep a closer eye on her, to find out what was going on.

Erica and Quan met up a few days later, at a small diner in a quiet part of town. It was their safe space, a place where they could be themselves. Quan could see the exhaustion in her eyes, the weight she carried. He reached across the table, taking her hand in his.

"You look tired," he said, his voice filled with concern. "Everything okay?"

Erica forced a smile, squeezing his hand. "Yeah, just work stuff. You know how it is."

Quan frowned, not buying it. He knew there was more to the story, but he didn't want to push her. He wanted her to open up on her own, to trust him. "You know you can talk to me, right? About anything."

Erica nodded, feeling a lump in her throat. She wanted to tell him everything, to spill her heart out. But she was scared, scared of what he would think, scared of losing him. She looked down, her voice barely a whisper. "I know. It's just... complicated."

Quan reached out, gently lifting her chin so she would look at him. "Hey, whatever it is, we'll figure it out. Together."

Erica felt tears prick her eyes. She nodded, swallowing the lump in her throat. "Yeah, together."

As they ate, Erica felt a warmth spread through her chest. Being with Quan felt right, like she was finally where she was meant to be. But there was always that nagging fear, the fear that Lil Ron would find out, that he would destroy everything. She pushed the thought aside, focusing on the moment. She wanted to hold on to this feeling, to the hope that maybe, just maybe, they could have a future together.

But Lil Ron wasn't one to be ignored. He started digging, asking around. He put a tail on Erica, watching her every move. It didn't take long for him to notice the changes. She was spending more time away from work, more time with this new guy. Ron didn't know who he was, but he didn't like it. Erica was his, and he wasn't about to let some nobody take her away.

One night, after Erica had finished with a client, Lil Ron showed up at her apartment. He was calm, too calm. Erica felt a chill run down her spine as he stepped inside, his eyes cold and calculating. He didn't say anything at first, just looked around, his gaze landing on the few personal items scattered about. A picture of her and Quan, a book he had lent her. Ron picked up the picture, his lips curling into a sneer.

"Who the fuck is this?" he asked, his voice low and dangerous.

Erica's heart pounded in her chest. She tried to play it off, to act nonchalant. "Just a friend."

Lil Ron's eyes narrowed. "A friend, huh? Funny, I ain't never seen you with any 'friends' before."

Erica swallowed hard, trying to keep her voice steady. "It's nothing, Ron. Just someone I met."

Ron dropped the picture, the glass shattering on the floor. Erica flinched, but Ron didn't react. He stepped closer, his eyes locked onto hers. "You better not be lyin' to me, Erica. You know how I feel about liars."

Erica nodded, her throat dry. "I'm not lyin'. It's nothin'."

Ron stared at her for a moment, his expression unreadable. Then he smiled, but it didn't reach his eyes. "Good. 'Cause if I find out you been keepin' shit from me, we gonna have a problem. You hear me?"

Erica nodded again, her heart racing. "Yeah, I hear you."

Ron took a step back, his smile fading. "Good. Now get some rest. We got a big client tomorrow."

He left without another word, leaving Erica standing in the shattered remains of the picture. She felt a wave of nausea, her legs shaking. She knew she was in deep, and the walls were closing in. Ron was onto her, and she didn't know how long she could keep up the charade. She wanted to run, to disappear with Quan and start over. But she knew it wasn't that simple. Ron had a hold on her, a grip she couldn't break.

As Erica cleaned up the broken glass, she felt a sense of despair. She was trapped, caught between two worlds. She wanted to be with Quan, to have a normal life. But she couldn't escape the reality of her situation. Ron would never let her go, and she couldn't risk putting Quan in danger. She felt tears welling up, but she quickly wiped them away. She couldn't afford to break down, not now.

She finished cleaning and sat on the edge of her bed, her mind racing. She knew she had to be careful, to keep her guard up. But the thought of losing Quan, of losing the chance at a normal life, was unbearable. She had to find a way out, a way to break free from Ron's grip. But for now, she had to play the game, had to keep up the facade.

As she lay down, Erica felt a sense of hopelessness. The life she wanted seemed so far out of reach, and the reality of her situation was closing in. She knew she had to be strong, to fight for what she wanted. But she also knew the risks, knew that one wrong move could destroy everything. As she closed her eyes, she felt a tear slip down her cheek. The double life she was living was tearing her apart, and she didn't know how much longer she could keep it up.

The streets were unforgiving, and Erica was caught in the crossfire. She had to be smart, had to be careful. But as she lay there, the weight of her choices pressing down on her, she knew that the path ahead was fraught with danger. The double life she was living was a dangerous game, and she was running out of time. She had to find a way out, before it was too late.

Chapter 5: The Turning Point

The moon hung low in the sky, casting an eerie glow over the city. Erica and Quan sat on the hood of his old car, parked in a quiet spot overlooking the skyline. The city lights flickered below, a constant reminder of the life Erica was trying to escape. She felt a knot in her stomach, knowing she had to tell Quan the truth. It was time to lay everything bare, to finally let him in on the reality of her life. She had been running from it for too long, hiding behind a facade. But she couldn't keep up the charade anymore. Not with him.

Quan sat beside her, his arm casually draped around her shoulders. He sensed her unease, felt the tension in her body. He turned to her, his eyes soft and filled with concern. "What's on your mind, Erica? You been actin' real distant lately."

Erica took a deep breath, steeling herself for what she was about to say. She looked down, her fingers nervously picking at the hem of her shirt. "Quan, there's somethin' I gotta tell you. Somethin' I been keepin' from you."

Quan's brow furrowed, his grip on her tightening slightly. "Aight, I'm listenin'."

Erica hesitated, feeling the weight of her confession pressing down on her. She had never been this vulnerable, never let anyone this close. But Quan deserved the truth, and she couldn't keep lying to him. She swallowed hard, her voice barely above a whisper. "I'm an escort, Quan. I been workin' for Lil Ron for years. He is my pimp. That's why I got all the nice stuff, the apartment, the clothes. It's all from that."

The words hung heavy in the air, the silence between them deafening. Erica felt her heart race, her stomach churning with anxiety. She braced herself for his reaction, expecting anger, disappointment, maybe even disgust. But Quan's face remained calm, his eyes locked onto hers.

After what felt like an eternity, Quan finally spoke, his voice low and steady. "I ain't gonna lie, that ain't what I expected. But it don't change how I feel 'bout you."

Erica blinked, her eyes widening in surprise. "It don't?"

Quan shook his head, a small smile tugging at the corners of his lips. "Nah. I ain't judgin' you, Erica. You did what you had to do to survive. I get that. But if you wanna leave that life, I'm here for you. We can get start over, start fresh."

Erica felt a wave of relief wash over her, tears pricking at the corners of her eyes. She had been so scared of losing him, of pushing him away with the truth. But here he was, standing by her, ready to help her escape. It felt like a weight had been lifted off her shoulders, a burden she had been carrying for far too long.

"You serious?" she asked, her voice trembling. "You really wanna help me get out?"

Quan nodded, his expression earnest. "Hell yeah, I'm serious. I ain't 'bout to let you go now."

Erica felt a tear slip down her cheek, quickly wiping it away. She looked at Quan, her heart swelling with emotion. He was offering her a way out, a chance at a new life. It was everything she had ever wanted, everything she had been too afraid to hope for.

They sat in silence for a moment, the gravity of the situation settling in. Erica knew it wouldn't be easy, that leaving Lil Ron wouldn't be as simple as walking away. He was possessive, controlling, and dangerous. He wouldn't let her go without a fight.

"So, what's the plan?" Erica asked, her voice steady despite the turmoil in her chest.

Quan leaned back, his eyes scanning the cityscape. "First, we gotta get you outta Lil Ron's grip. He ain't gonna let you go easy, so we gotta be smart 'bout this. We can save up, get enough cash to start over somewhere new. I got some connects who can help us disappear, and if needed get new identities and shit."

Erica nodded, her mind racing with possibilities. It was risky, but it was their only chance. She thought about all the times she had dreamed of a normal life, a life away from the streets. This was her shot, and she wasn't going to let it slip away.

"We gotta be careful," Erica said, her voice firm. "Lil Ron got eyes everywhere. If he finds out we tryna leave, he won't just let it slide. We gotta do this right, no mistakes."

Quan nodded in agreement. "Yeah, I know. We gotta play it cool, keep up appearances. You gotta keep workin' for now, make him think everything's normal. Meanwhile, I'll start makin' arrangements, get us set up for the move."

Erica felt a chill run down her spine at the thought of continuing her work with Lil Ron. They couldn't afford to arouse his suspicions. She had to keep up the facade, at least for a little while longer.

"Okay," she said, her voice resolute. "We can do this. We just gotta be smart 'bout it."

Quan smiled, his eyes filled with determination. "Damn right we can. We gonna get outta this mess, Erica. We gonna start a new life, away from all this bullshit."

Erica felt a surge of hope, a sense of purpose she hadn't felt in years. She looked at Quan, feeling a deep sense of gratitude and love. He was her lifeline, her anchor in the storm. With him, she felt like she could take on the world.

As they sat there, wrapped in each other's arms, Erica felt a newfound resolve. She was done being a pawn in Lil Ron's game. She was ready to take control of her life, to break free from the chains that bound her. It wouldn't be easy, and it wouldn't be without risks. But she was ready to fight with everything in her.

The night wore on, the city lights twinkling in the distance. Erica and Quan continued to talk, making plans and dreaming of the future. They knew the road ahead would be tough, filled with obstacles and dangers. But they were ready to face it together. They had each other, and that was enough.

As they finally decided to head back, Erica felt a sense of peace wash over her. For the first time in a long time, she felt hopeful, excited for the future. She knew there would be challenges, that Lil Ron wouldn't let her go easily. But she also knew she had Quan by her side, and together, they could overcome anything.

As they drove back to her apartment, Erica felt a mixture of fear and excitement. She knew she was stepping into dangerous territory, that the path they were taking was fraught with risks. But she was ready to take the leap, to fight for the life she deserved. She was ready to leave the darkness behind and step into the light.

The car pulled up to her building, and Quan walked her to the door. They stood there for a moment, wrapped in each other's embrace. Erica felt a sense of comfort and safety in his arms, a feeling she had never known before.

"Thank you, Quan," she whispered, her voice choked with emotion. "For everything."

Quan smiled, his eyes soft and warm. "Ain't nothin', Erica. We in this together, remember?"

Erica nodded, her heart full. She leaned in, pressing her lips to his in a gentle kiss. It was a promise, a vow to stand by each other no matter what. As they pulled away, Erica felt a surge of determination. She was ready to face whatever came their way, ready to fight for their future.

As she watched him drive away, Erica felt a sense of calm. It was a turning point, the beginning of a new chapter in her life. She was done being a victim, done being controlled. She was ready to take control of her destiny, to carve out a new path.

As she walked into her apartment, Erica felt a sense of anticipation. She knew the risks, knew the dangers. But she also knew that she was finally on the path to freedom. The life she wanted was within reach, and she was ready to grab it with both hands. It was a dangerous game, but Erica was ready to play. And this time, she was determined to win.

Chapter 6: Lil Ron's Discovery

The streets were quiet, the usual hustle and bustle replaced by the eerie stillness of the late night. Erica had just left Quan's place, her heart full of the promise of a new beginning. She felt a strange mix of excitement and fear, the thrill of their plans tempered by the looming danger of Lil Ron. As she walked down the dimly lit sidewalk, she couldn't shake the feeling of being watched. It was a paranoia she couldn't quite place, but it gnawed at her nonetheless.

Unbeknownst to Erica, Lil Ron had been keeping tabs on her for weeks. His suspicions had grown, fueled by her increasing absences and the changes in her demeanor. He had always been possessive, but now he was paranoid, convinced she was hiding something. And Lil Ron didn't like being kept in the dark. So, he decided to follow her, to see for himself what she was up to.

That night, Lil Ron sat in his car, parked a few blocks away from Quan's apartment. He watched as Erica stepped out, her face glowing with a happiness he hadn't seen in a long time. It made his blood boil. He knew that look; it was the look of a woman in love. A woman planning to escape. His jaw clenched, a wave of fury washing over him. He had given her everything, and this was how she repaid him? By sneaking around with some nobody?

As Erica walked, she felt a chill run down her spine. She quickened her pace, her instincts screaming at her to get off the streets. She reached her apartment building and hurried inside, locking the door behind her. She leaned against it, trying to steady her breathing. She couldn't shake the feeling that something was about to go very wrong.

She was right.

The next day, Lil Ron showed up at Erica's apartment unannounced. She opened the door to find him standing there, his expression cold and menacing. Her heart sank, a wave of fear crashing over her. She knew this wasn't a social call. Lil Ron pushed past her, making himself at home. He didn't say anything at first, just looked around the apartment, his eyes cold and calculating.

Erica stood there, her hands trembling. She knew she had to play it cool, had to act like everything was normal. "What's up, Ron? You lookin' for somethin'?"

Lil Ron turned to face her, his eyes narrowing. "Yeah, I'm lookin' for the truth. You been actin' real funny lately, Erica. Skippin' out on work, sneakin' around. You got somethin' you wanna tell me?"

Erica's heart raced, her mind scrambling for an excuse. "I been busy, that's all. Just tryin' to take care of some personal stuff."

Lil Ron's lip curled into a sneer. "Personal stuff, huh? Like that dude you been seein'? The one you think I don't know 'bout?"

Erica felt her blood run cold. He knew. She tried to keep her face neutral, but she couldn't hide the fear in her eyes. "I don't know what you talkin' 'bout, Ron."

Lil Ron took a step closer, his voice low and dangerous. "Don't play dumb with me, Erica. I followed you last night. I saw you with him. You think you can just sneak around behind my back and get away with it?"

Erica's mind raced, her thoughts a chaotic mess. She knew Lil Ron was dangerous, knew what he was capable of. But she couldn't back down now. She had to stand her ground. "I ain't sneakin' around. And what I do on my own time ain't none of your business."

Lil Ron's eyes flashed with anger. He grabbed her arm, pulling her close. "You think you can talk to me like that? You forget who you work for? You belong to me, Erica. You ain't goin' nowhere without my say-so."

Erica winced, the pain in her arm sharp and sudden. She tried to pull away, but his grip was like a vice. "Let go of me, Ron. Don't do this."

Lil Ron's grip tightened, his voice a deadly whisper. "Oh, I can do whatever the fuck I want. And if you think you can just walk away, you got another thing comin'. You leave, and I'll make sure that pretty boy of yours gets what's comin' to him. You understand me?"

Erica felt a surge of panic. She knew he meant it. Lil Ron wasn't the type to make idle threats. She struggled to keep her composure, to hide the fear that threatened to overwhelm her. "You wouldn't dare."

Lil Ron chuckled, a dark, menacing sound. "Try me. You know I don't play, Erica. You try to leave, and I'll make sure both of you pay. You ain't nothin' without me. You think you can run off and start fresh? You think he'll want you when he finds out what you really are?"

Tears welled up in Erica's eyes, but she refused to let them fall. She wouldn't give him the satisfaction. "You don't own me, Ron. I ain't your property."

Lil Ron's eyes narrowed, his grip on her arm painfully tight. "No, but you owe me. I made you, and I can break you just as easy. You think you're better than this, better than me? You ain't nothin' but a whore, Erica. And that's all you'll ever be."

Erica felt a tear slip down her cheek, quickly wiping it away. She knew she was trapped, caught in Lil Ron's web. But she couldn't let him win. She had to find a way out, to protect Quan and herself. "Just leave, Ron. Please."

Lil Ron stared at her for a moment, his expression cold and unreadable. Then he let go of her arm, stepping back. "Fine. But don't think this is over. You try to leave, and I'll make sure you regret it. You belong to me, Erica. And I don't let go of what's mine."

With that, he turned and walked out, slamming the door behind him. Erica collapsed onto the floor, her body trembling. She felt a wave of relief and terror wash over her. Lil Ron knew about Quan, and he wasn't going to let her go without a fight. She knew she had to act fast, to find a way to escape before it was too late.

As she sat there, tears streaming down her face, Erica felt a surge of determination. She couldn't let Lil Ron control her life any longer. She had to protect Quan, had to protect herself. She had to find a way out, to break free.

The room felt cold and empty, the silence oppressive. Erica knew she was on borrowed time, that Lil Ron wouldn't hesitate to hurt them if he felt threatened. She had to act fast, to make a plan. She couldn't let fear paralyze her. She had to be strong, for herself and for Quan.

Erica wiped away her tears, her mind racing. She knew the risks, knew the dangers. But she was ready to fight, ready to do whatever it took. She wouldn't let Lil Ron win. She wouldn't let him destroy the one chance she had at a better life.

As she stood up, Erica felt a sense of resolve wash over her. She was over it!

The city lights flickered outside, a reminder of the life she was desperate to escape. Erica knew the fight was just beginning, that Lil Ron wouldn't back down without a battle. Was she ready to face him? Ready to stand up for herself? She was done hiding, done running. It was time to take a stand.

As the night wore on, Erica felt a sense of calm settle over her. She knew the risks, knew the dangers. But she was ready to fight, ready to take control of her life. Lil Ron had pushed her too far, and now she was ready to push back. She wouldn't let him win. She wouldn't let him destroy her.

Chapter 7: The Fear Sets In

The days that followed Lil Ron's confrontation were a blur for Erica. She felt like she was walking on a tightrope, the ground below filled with jagged rocks waiting to tear her apart. The fear gnawed at her, a constant, unrelenting presence. Every shadow felt like a threat, every knock on the door a potential danger. She was trapped in a nightmare, torn between her love for Quan and the looming terror of Lil Ron's wrath.

Erica sat in her apartment; the silence eerie. The city noises outside felt distant, muted. She clutched her phone, Quan's number displayed on the screen. She hadn't told him about Lil Ron's threats yet, afraid of dragging him deeper into her mess. She knew she couldn't hide the truth forever, but the thought of losing Quan, of putting him in danger, was unbearable.

Her thoughts were interrupted by a knock on the door. Erica's heart raced, her body tensing. She moved cautiously, peering through the peephole. Relief washed over her as she saw Quan standing there, a concerned expression on his face. She quickly unlocked the door, pulling him inside.

"Hey, what's wrong?" Quan asked, his eyes scanning her face. He could see the fear in her eyes, the way her hands trembled. It broke his heart to see her like this.

Erica closed the door, locking it behind them. She turned to him, her eyes filled with unshed tears. "It's Ron... he knows 'bout us. He confronted me, threatened me. He said if I tried to leave, he'd come after you."

Quan's expression darkened, his jaw clenching. He pulled her into his arms, holding her close. "Ain't nothin' gonna happen to you, Erica. I won't let him touch you."

Erica buried her face in his chest, her tears finally spilling over. She clung to him, feeling a mix of fear and love. She wanted to believe him, to trust that everything would be okay. But the reality of their situation loomed over them, a dark cloud that refused to dissipate.

Quan gently pulled back, cupping her face in his hands. "We gonna get through this, I promise. I ain't gonna let no one hurt you. We just gotta stick to the plan, keep our heads down."

Erica looked up at him, her eyes filled with uncertainty. "But what if he finds out we tryna leave? What if he comes after you?"

Quan shook his head, his eyes fierce. "I ain't scared of him. He ain't got no power over me. We gonna leave this place, start fresh. Ain't nothin' he can do to stop us."

Erica felt a surge of hope, a glimmer of light in the darkness. Quan's confidence was reassuring, a beacon of strength she desperately needed. She nodded, trying to steady her breathing. "Okay. We stick to the plan. But we gotta be careful, Quan. Ron's dangerous. He'll do whatever it takes to keep me under his thumb."

Quan nodded, his expression serious. "I know. But we ain't alone. I got people who can help us, get us outta this mess. We just gotta be patient, play it smart."

They sat down on the couch, Erica leaning into Quan's side. She felt a sense of comfort in his presence, a feeling of safety she hadn't felt in a long time. They had talked about their plans, about the life they wanted to build together. It felt like a dream, so close yet so far away. But with Quan by her side, Erica felt like they could make it a reality.

As the night wore on, Erica felt a sense of calm settle over her. Quan's reassurance was like a balm to her frayed nerves. She knew the road ahead would be tough, filled with obstacles and dangers. But she was ready to face it, ready to fight for their future. She couldn't let fear dictate her life.

But deep down, the fear lingered. It was a shadow that followed her everywhere, a reminder of the danger they were in. Erica knew she had to stay strong, for herself and for Quan. She couldn't let Lil Ron control her life any longer. She had to break free, to escape the grasps of this life.

The next morning, Erica woke up with a renewed sense of purpose. She was done being a victim, done being afraid. She and Quan had a plan, and they were going to see it through. She got dressed, ready to face whatever the day threw at her.

As she left her apartment, Erica felt the familiar knot of anxiety in her stomach. She knew Lil Ron would be watching her, waiting for any sign of betrayal. She had to be careful, had to keep up the facade. But as she walked down the street, she couldn't shake the feeling of eyes on her, the weight of the danger that loomed over them.

At work, Erica went through the motions, her mind elsewhere. Lil Ron was his usual self, cold and controlling. He watched her closely, his eyes filled with suspicion. Erica did her best to act normal, to hide the fear that gnawed at her insides. But every interaction felt like a test, a dangerous game of cat and mouse.

After work, Erica met up with Quan. They went to a quiet café, away from prying eyes. They sat in a corner booth, speaking in hushed tones. Quan updated her on their progress, the arrangements he was making to get them out of the city. It was a risky plan, but it was their only shot.

As they left the café, Erica felt a sense of resolve. She was done being afraid, done being controlled. She was ready to take control of her life and go after the life she knew she deserved. A life full of happiness.

But as they walked down the street, Erica felt a shiver run down her spine. She glanced around, her eyes scanning the shadows. She couldn't shake the feeling of being watched, the sense of danger that hung in the air. She gripped Quan's hand tighter, her heart racing.

Quan noticed her tension, his expression concerned. "You okay?"

Erica nodded, forcing a smile. "Yeah, just... nervous."

Quan pulled her closer, his arm around her shoulders. "Don't worry. We got this."

Erica nodded, trying to push down the fear that threatened to overwhelm her. She had to be strong, had to stay focused. But the fear was like a shadow, always there, always lurking. She knew they had to move fast, to get out before Lil Ron made his move.

As they reached her apartment, Erica felt a sense of relief. She hugged Quan tightly, feeling his warmth and strength. He kissed her forehead, his voice soft. "We'll get through this, Erica. I promise."

Erica nodded, her eyes filled with determination. "I know. I believe you."

They stood there for a moment, holding each other close. Erica felt a sense of calm wash over her, a fleeting moment of peace in the storm. She knew the road ahead would be tough, but she was ready to face it.

As she watched him leave, Erica felt a surge of emotion. She was scared, yes, but she was also hopeful. They had a plan, a way out. They just had to stay strong, to keep moving forward. The fear was still there, but Erica refused to let it control her. She was ready to fight for her future, for the life she wanted.

Chapter 8: Lil Ron's Retaliation

The city was alive with its usual chaos, but for Erica, every shadow seemed darker, every alleyway more threatening. She and Quan had tried to maintain a low profile, sticking to their plan to escape Lil Ron's clutches. But no matter how careful they were, Lil Ron's presence loomed over them like a specter. It was only a matter of time before he made his move, and Erica knew it would be brutal.

Lil Ron had always been possessive, but now he was enraged. Erica's attempt to leave his grip had wounded his pride, and he was determined to make her pay. He started showing up at places he knew she'd be, watching her from a distance. His eyes were cold, calculating, filled with a promise of violence. He made it clear that he wasn't done with her, not by a long shot.

Erica first noticed him outside the café where she and Quan had their secret meetings. He stood across the street, leaning against a lamppost, his eyes locked onto her. She got goosebumps, her breath catching in her throat. She quickly ducked inside, her heart pounding. She knew he was trying to intimidate her, to make her feel trapped. And it was working.

As the days passed, Lil Ron's presence became more intrusive. He started following Erica, tailing her wherever she went. He'd park outside her apartment building, his car a menacing reminder of the danger she was in. He even showed up at Quan's place, leaving threatening messages scrawled on the car. "You can't hide from me," one read. Another simply said, "She's mine."

The constant surveillance was suffocating. Erica felt like a prisoner in her own life, unable to escape Lil Ron's grasp. She tried to keep up appearances, to act normal, but the fear was always there, lurking beneath the surface. She confided in Quan, telling him about Lil Ron's threats and how he was stalking them. Quan was furious, but also scared for her. He wanted to confront Lil Ron, to put an end to the harassment, but Erica begged him not to. She knew it would only make things worse.

One night, after a particularly tense day, Erica returned to her apartment to find Lil Ron waiting for her. He stood in the hallway, his face a mask of cold rage. Erica froze, her keys slipping from her fingers. She knew she was trapped, nowhere to run.

"Thought you could hide from me, huh?" Lil Ron's voice was low, dangerous. He stepped closer, his eyes boring into hers. "You think you can just walk away? From me?"

Erica tried to muster the courage to stand up to him, but her voice came out shaky. "Ron, please. Just leave me alone."

Lil Ron's lip curled into a sneer. "Leave you alone? Bitch, you belong to me. You think you can just fuck around with some punk-ass nigga and get away with it?"

Before Erica could react, Lil Ron grabbed her by the arm, yanking her towards him. The force of his grip made her gasp in pain. She tried to pull away, but he was too strong. "You think you can disrespect me like this?" he snarled, his face inches from hers. "You got no idea who you fuckin' with."

Erica felt the first blow before she even saw it coming. Lil Ron's fist connected with her jaw, sending her crashing to the floor. Pain exploded in her head, her vision blurring. She tried to scramble away, but Lil Ron was on her, raining down blows. His fists were relentless, each one punctuated by his angry shouts.

"You think you're better than me?" he spat, his voice filled with venom. "You ain't shit without me. You hear me?"

Erica tried to curl into a ball, to protect herself, but the pain was overwhelming. She could taste blood, feel it trickling down her face. Her head was spinning, her body screaming in agony. She felt a tear slip down her cheek, a sob escaping her lips.

Lil Ron finally stopped, breathing heavily. He stood over her, his chest heaving with rage. Erica lay on the floor, barely able to move. She looked up at him, her vision swimming. He glared down at her, his eyes cold and unforgiving.

"Don't you ever try to leave me again," he hissed, his voice deadly quiet. "Or I'll make sure you and that nigga both pay. You got that?"

Erica nodded weakly, tears streaming down her face. She could barely speak, her jaw throbbing in pain. "Yes," she whispered, her voice barely audible.

Lil Ron stepped back, satisfied. He straightened his jacket, his expression shifting to one of cold indifference. "Good. Now clean yourself up. You got work tomorrow."

With that, he turned and walked away, leaving Erica lying on the floor, broken and bruised. She lay there for a moment, unable to move. The pain was excruciating, her body screaming in agony. She felt a wave of despair wash over her, the reality of her situation sinking in. She was trapped, a prisoner in Lil Ron's twisted game. And there was no way out.

As the adrenaline wore off, Erica managed to pull herself up. She stumbled to the bathroom, wincing at every step. She looked in the mirror, barely recognizing the battered face staring back at her. Her lip was split, her eye swollen, bruises already forming on her cheek. She felt a wave of nausea, the room spinning around her.

She turned on the faucet, splashing cold water on her face. The water stung her wounds, but she didn't care. She needed to feel something, anything other than the overwhelming fear and pain. She gripped the sink, her knuckles white. She had to get out. She had to find a way to escape Lil Ron's clutches. But how? He had made it clear that he would never let her go.

Erica sank to the floor, her body shaking with sobs. She felt a sense of hopelessness, a dark cloud that threatened to swallow her whole. She couldn't go on like this, living in constant fear, under Lil Ron's control. She wanted to be free, to live her life without looking over her shoulder. But that dream felt so far away, a distant fantasy.

As she sat there, broken and defeated, Erica thought of Quan. He was her lifeline, her hope. But she couldn't drag him into this mess. Lil Ron had made it clear that he would go after him if she tried to leave. She couldn't bear the thought of something happening to Quan because of her. She had to protect him, even if it meant staying in this hell.

The city outside was still bustling, the noise a distant hum. But for Erica, the world had shrunk to the small, cold bathroom where she sat. She felt the weight of her situation pressing down on her, the fear and pain a constant presence.

As she finally stood up, Erica looked at her reflection one last time. She saw the bruises, the blood, the pain. But she also saw something else—determination. She wasn't done fighting. Not yet. She would find a way out, a way to escape Lil Ron's twisted game. She had to. For herself, for Quan, for the future she so desperately wanted. But how?

Chapter 9: The Breaking Point

The morning after Lil Ron's brutal attack, Erica woke up feeling like she had been hit by a freight train. Every part of her body ached, her face swollen and bruised. She lay in bed, staring at the ceiling, her mind racing. The events of the previous night played over and over in her head, a twisted nightmare she couldn't escape. She felt trapped, cornered by Lil Ron's threats and violence. The weight of the situation pressed down on her, suffocating her.

Quan had called her multiple times, worried sick when she didn't pick up. She finally managed to muster the strength to grab her phone and text him. She didn't want him to see her like this, but she knew she couldn't avoid him forever. Her hands shook as she typed, trying to keep her message short and vague.

Erica: *Hey, I'm okay. Just need some time. I'll call you later.*

She sent the message and tossed the phone aside, feeling a fresh wave of tears welling up. She knew she couldn't keep lying to him, couldn't keep hiding the truth. But she also knew that telling him would only put him in more danger. Lil Ron had made it clear that he wouldn't hesitate to hurt Quan if she tried to leave.

Erica spent the rest of the day in a daze, her body sore and her mind numb. She couldn't stop thinking about what Lil Ron had said, the threats he had made. She knew he was serious, that he wouldn't stop until he had total control over her again.

As the day turned into night, Erica's anxiety grew. She knew she needed to talk to Quan, to figure out their next move. But the thought of dragging him deeper into this mess made her feel sick. She couldn't bear the thought of something happening to him because of her. She had to protect him, even if it meant sacrificing her own self.

Erica finally picked up her phone and called Quan. He answered on the first ring, his voice filled with concern. "Erica, where the hell you been? I been worried sick."

She took a deep breath, trying to keep her voice steady. "I'm sorry, Quan. I just... needed some time."

"What's goin' on? You sound off," Quan pressed, his tone anxious.

Erica hesitated, her mind racing. She knew she had to tell him the truth, but the words felt like a weight in her chest. "Ron came by last night," she finally said, her voice barely above a whisper. "He... He ain't happy, Quan. He threatened you, said he'd come after you if I tried to leave."

There was a long pause on the other end of the line. When Quan finally spoke, his voice was low and furious. "That motherfucker. What'd he do to you, Erica?"

Erica swallowed hard, feeling a lump in her throat. "He... he hurt me, Quan. But I'll be okay. I just... I don't know what to do."

Quan's voice softened, filled with concern. "You ain't goin' back to him. I won't let you."

Erica felt tears in her eyes, her heart aching. "But what if he hurts you? I can't let that happen, Quan. Maybe... maybe I should just go back, keep him off our backs."

"Fuck that," Quan snapped, his voice sharp. "You ain't goin' back to that piece of shit. I don't care what he says. We gonna find a way out, Erica. We just gotta stick together."

Erica's resolve wavered, the fear gnawing at her. She wanted to believe him, to trust that they could escape. But the reality of their situation felt insurmountable. "Quan, you don't understand. Ron ain't gonna let this go. He'll do whatever it takes to keep me under his thumb. I don't want you to get hurt because of me."

"Fuck Him!"," Quan shouted, his voice firm. "You worth fightin' for, Erica. I ain't givin' up on you, and you ain't givin' up on me. We in this together, no matter what."

Erica felt a sob escape her lips, her body shaking with emotion. She knew he was right, that they couldn't let fear dictate their lives. But the thought of Lil Ron's wrath, the danger they were in, was overwhelming.

She felt torn, trapped between her love for Quan and the fear of what Lil Ron might do.

"Okay," she finally whispered, her voice trembling. "We stick to the plan. But we gotta be careful, Quan. Ron's dangerous. We can't take any chances."

Quan's voice softened, filled with determination. "We got this, baby. We gonna get through this. Just trust me."

Erica nodded, wiping away her tears. She knew she had to trust him, had to believe that they could make it out of this nightmare. But the fear was still there, a dark cloud that loomed over them. She couldn't shake the feeling that something terrible was about to happen.

The days that followed were tense, filled with a sense of impending doom. Erica and Quan continued to make plans, trying to stay one step ahead of Lil Ron. They kept their meetings discreet, careful not to draw any attention. But the fear was always there, lurking in the shadows. Erica couldn't shake the feeling of being watched, of Lil Ron's eyes on her.

One night, as Erica sat in her apartment, she heard a knock on the door. Her heart raced, her body tensing. She slowly approached the door, peering through the peephole. It was Quan. She quickly unlocked the door, pulling him inside.

"We need to talk," Quan said, his voice urgent. He looked around, as if expecting Lil Ron to appear at any moment. "I been thinkin'. We gotta leave, like, now. We can't wait no more."

Erica felt a surge of panic. "But we ain't ready yet. We ain't got everything we need."

Quan shook his head, his expression grim. "We ain't got time to be ready. We gotta go, before it's too late. I got a friend who can help us, get us outta the city. We just gotta move fast."

Erica felt a lump form in her throat, her mind racing. She knew he was right, that they couldn't wait any longer. But the thought of leaving everything behind, of starting over, was terrifying. She felt like she was standing on the edge of a cliff, staring into the abyss.

"Okay," she finally whispered, her voice shaky. "Let's do it. Let's get outta here."

Quan pulled her into his arms, holding her tight. "We gonna be okay, Erica."

Erica nodded, feeling a mix of fear and hope.

Chapter 10: The Plan to Escape

The city buzzed with its usual chaos, but for Erica and Quan, it felt like a pressure cooker about to explode. Every corner they turned, every shadow felt like Lil Ron's looming presence. They knew they were running out of time. The plan to escape was no longer a distant idea but a necessary action. It was now or never.

Erica sat on the edge of Quan's bed, her face still bruised and swollen from Lil Ron's attack. Her eyes were red from lack of sleep, her nerves frayed. Quan paced the small apartment, the tension in the air palpable. He had a friend, an old contact from his hustling days, who could help them disappear. But it was risky, and the clock was ticking.

"We gotta move fast," Quan muttered, his voice low and urgent. "I called up Smoke. He says he can hook us up with IDs, new names, the whole package. But we gotta meet him tonight."

Erica nodded, her stomach in knots. "How much we need?"

Quan stopped pacing and looked at her, his expression grim. "A lot. But I got some saved up. We can pawn some shit, get the rest. Smoke don't work for free, and he ain't the type to cut deals."

Erica swallowed hard, feeling the weight of their situation. They were about to jump into the unknown, leaving everything behind. The thought was terrifying, but staying was not an option. "Okay, let's do it. We pawn whatever we got, get the cash, and meet Smoke. We gotta get outta here, Quan. I can't take another day of this."

Quan walked over to her, his eyes filled with determination. "We gonna make it, Erica. We gonna get outta this hellhole and start fresh. Just gotta keep our heads straight."

They spent the next few hours gathering whatever they could sell. Jewelry, electronics, anything of value. It felt surreal, like they were in a movie, playing out a desperate escape plan. They moved quickly, not wanting to linger in one place for too long. The fear of Lil Ron catching wind of their plan was a constant shadow.

As they gathered their things, Erica couldn't help but think about the life they were leaving behind. It wasn't much, but it was all she knew. The streets, the hustle, the constant grind. It was a hard life, but it was her life. The thought of starting over, somewhere new, was both exhilarating and terrifying. But she knew they had no choice. Lil Ron wouldn't stop until he had her back under his control.

They loaded the items into Quan's car, driving to a pawn shop in a seedy part of town. The place was a dump, but they didn't have time to be picky. Quan handled the negotiations, his voice low and steady. The pawnshop owner, a grizzled old man with a cigarette dangling from his lips, eyed them suspiciously but eventually handed over the cash. It wasn't much, but it was enough to get them started.

With the money in hand, they drove to a rundown warehouse on the outskirts of the city. The place was a relic, abandoned and forgotten. Quan parked the car, his fingers tapping nervously on the steering wheel. Erica felt her heart race, her hands clammy. This was it. There was no turning back.

Smoke was waiting for them inside, a tall, wiry man with a face that spoke of hard times. His eyes were sharp, calculating, taking in every detail. He greeted Quan with a nod, his gaze flicking to Erica. "So, this the girl you riskin' it all for, huh?"

Quan stiffened, his jaw clenched. "Yeah, this is Erica. We need out, Smoke. New names, IDs, everything."

Smoke smirked, his eyes glinting with amusement. "Aight, I can do that. But it ain't cheap. You got the cash?"

Quan handed over the money, his expression tense. "All of it. Every penny we got."

Smoke counted the cash, nodding in satisfaction. "Good. You smart to come to me. Most people don't make it outta this life. But I can give you a fresh start. New names, new IDs, the works. Just don't come cryin' to me if shit goes south."

Erica felt a chill run down her spine. She knew this was dangerous, that they were putting their lives in the hands of a man they barely knew. But they had no other choice. She looked at Smoke, her voice steady. "We just want out. We ain't lookin' to cause trouble."

Smoke chuckled, a sound that sent a shiver through her. "Trouble's part of the package, sweetheart. But I'll do my best to make sure you disappear. Just remember, once you gone, you gone. Ain't no comin' back."

Quan nodded, his eyes hard. "We know. Just do your thing."

Smoke pulled out a small black bag, setting it on the table. He opened it, revealing a laptop and a portable scanner. "Aight, let's get this done. I need new photos, new everything. You got any preference for names?"

Erica and Quan exchanged a look, a silent conversation passing between them. "No preference," Quan said finally. "Just make sure they ain't traceable."

Smoke nodded, his fingers flying over the keyboard. He worked quickly, efficiently, the air filled with the soft hum of the laptop. Erica felt a knot of anxiety in her stomach, the reality of what they were doing sinking in. They were erasing themselves, leaving behind everything they knew. It was both liberating and terrifying.

As Smoke worked, Erica couldn't help but think about the dangers they faced. Lil Ron was ruthless, and if he found out what they were planning, there would be hell to pay. She tried to push the thoughts aside, focusing on the future. A new life, a fresh start. It was all she had ever wanted, but the price was high.

After what felt like an eternity, Smoke finished. He handed them each a set of IDs, complete with new names and photos. Erica looked at hers, feeling a strange sense of detachment. It was her face, but the name was foreign. It was like looking at a stranger. She glanced at Quan, who was staring at his own ID with a similar expression.

Smoke packed up his equipment, his expression businesslike. "There you go. You two are officially off the grid. But remember, this shit ain't foolproof. You gotta lay low, stay outta trouble. You mess up, and you're on your own."

Quan nodded, his voice firm. "We know. Thanks, Smoke."

Smoke waved a hand dismissively. "Just doin' my job. Now get outta here before you draw attention. And good luck. You gonna need it."

Erica and Quan left the warehouse, the weight of their new identities pressing down on them. They got back into the car, the silence heavy. Erica clutched her new ID, her mind racing. They were almost free, but at what cost? The fear of Lil Ron's retaliation still lingered, a dark cloud that refused to dissipate.

As they drove away, Quan reached over and squeezed her hand. "We are doing it, Erica. We gettin out. Now we just gotta stay outta sight, start over."

Erica nodded, a lump forming in her throat. "Yeah. But we gotta be careful, Quan. Ron ain't gonna let this go. We can't make any mistakes."

Quan's expression was determined, his eyes hard. "We won't. We gonna make it, Erica. We just gotta stay strong."

Erica felt a flicker of hope, a small spark in the darkness. They had done it. They had taken the first step towards a new life. But the road ahead was uncertain, filled with dangers and unknowns. She knew they couldn't afford to let their guard down, not even for a moment.

As they drove into the night, leaving the city behind, Erica felt a mix of emotions. Fear, hope, relief. They were free, but they were also fugitives, running from a past that refused to let them go. The future was a blank slate, filled with possibilities and risks. But for the first time in a long time, Erica felt like she could breathe.

They had a long way to go, and the road would be tough. But they had each other, and that was enough. Erica looked at Quan, feeling a surge of love and determination. They would make it. They had to. They were free, and nothing could stop them now.

The city lights faded into the distance, and with them, the shadows of their past. Erica felt a sense of closure, a chapter of her life coming to an end. But as one door closed, another opened. The future was uncertain, but it was theirs to create. And Erica was ready to face it, head-on.

Chapter 11: The Failed Escape

The city was a labyrinth of streets and secrets, and Erica and Quan were determined to escape its grasp. They had everything they needed: new identities, enough cash to get by, and a plan to leave it all behind. The air was thick with anticipation as they made their way through the darkened alleys, their footsteps echoing in the silence. The night was their ally, cloaking them in shadows as they navigated the dangerous path to freedom.

Erica's heart pounded in her chest, each beat a reminder of the life she was leaving behind. The bruises on her face were a painful testament to Lil Ron's wrath, a stark reminder of the dangers they faced. She glanced at Quan, his face set in determination. They had to get out, had to break free from the chains that bound them. But as they approached the rendezvous point, a sense of unease settled over her. Something felt off, a nagging suspicion that they weren't as alone as they thought.

Quan pulled the car into a deserted parking lot, the only light coming from a flickering streetlamp.

"Something ain't right," Quan muttered, his eyes scanning the shadows. His hand instinctively reached for the gun tucked into his waistband, a precaution they had hoped they wouldn't need.

Erica nodded, her pulse quickening. She felt the weight of their decision pressing down on her, the fear of what lay ahead. She was about to say something when the sound of tires screeching cut through the silence. Her heart dropped as a black SUV sped into the lot, skidding to a halt a few feet away. The doors flew open, and out stepped Lil Ron, flanked by a couple of his goons.

Erica's blood ran cold. Lil Ron's eyes were locked onto hers, a cruel smile spreading across his face. He looked every bit the predator, relishing the fear he saw in her eyes. "Well, well, look who we got here," he drawled, his voice dripping with malice. "Y'all really thought you could just leave me, huh? You must be outta your damn minds."

Quan stepped in front of Erica, his hand on the grip of his gun. "Back off, Ron. We ain't lookin' for trouble. Just let us go."

Lil Ron chuckled, a dark, menacing sound. He shook his head, his gaze shifting to Quan. "You think you can just take my property and walk away? You got some nerve, boy."

Erica felt a surge of anger, her fear momentarily eclipsed by her hatred for Lil Ron. "I ain't your property, Ron. You don't own me."

Lil Ron's expression darkened, his eyes narrowing. He took a step closer, his voice cold. "You got some mouth on you, girl. Maybe I need to remind you who you belong to."

Before anyone could react, one of Lil Ron's goons lunged at Quan. The two men grappled, the sound of grunts and fists flying filling the air. Erica watched in horror as Quan fought to defend himself, his back against the car. She felt a surge of panic, her eyes darting around for a way out.

Without thinking, Erica reached into the car and grabbed the gun they had stashed in the glove compartment. Her hands trembled as she aimed it at Lil Ron, her finger hovering over the trigger. "Stop! Or I'll shoot."

Lil Ron turned to her, a look of surprise flickering across his face. Then he laughed, a cruel, mocking sound. "You ain't got the guts, girl. You ain't never had the guts."

Erica's hands shook, the weight of the gun heavy in her grasp. She knew he was right. She had never been the type to resort to violence, to hurt someone. But as she looked at Quan, struggling to fend off the goon, she felt a surge of anger. She couldn't let Ron win. She couldn't let him take everything from her.

With a deep breath, Erica steadied her aim. "Let him go, Ron. Now."

Lil Ron's smile faded, replaced by a cold, calculating look. He took a step closer, his hands raised in a mock gesture of surrender. "Aight, aight. No need to get all worked up. We can work this out."

Erica kept the gun trained on him, her heart racing. She didn't trust him, not for a second. "Get back in your car and leave. Now."

For a moment, it seemed like Ron would comply. He glanced at his goons, a silent signal passing between them. Then, in a flash, he lunged at Erica, knocking the gun from her hands. The weapon skittered across the pavement, out of reach. Erica stumbled back, her breath catching in her throat.

Lil Ron grabbed her by the arm, his grip like a vice. "You think you can just pull a gun on me?" he snarled, his face inches from hers. "You got a lot to learn, bitch."

Before Erica could react, Quan broke free from his assailant and tackled Lil Ron to the ground. The two men wrestled, fists flying in a flurry of violence. Erica scrambled to her feet, her mind racing. She had to do something, had to help Quan. She spotted the gun lying a few feet away and dove for it, her fingers closing around the grip.

Without thinking, she aimed the gun at Lil Ron, her hands shaking. "Get off him! Now!"

Lil Ron looked up, his eyes filled with rage. He hesitated, then slowly released Quan, raising his hands in surrender. Erica kept the gun pointed at him, her heart pounding. She knew they had only seconds to escape.

"Let's go!" she shouted at Quan, backing towards the car.

Quan didn't need to be told twice. He scrambled to his feet, blood trickling from a cut on his forehead. He grabbed Erica's hand, pulling her towards the car. They jumped in, slamming the doors shut. Erica's hands fumbled with the keys, her adrenaline making her movements clumsy. The engine roared to life, and Quan hit the gas, the car lurching forward.

As they sped out of the parking lot, Erica glanced back, her heart in her throat. Lil Ron stood there, watching them go, a dark, menacing figure silhouetted against the night. She knew this wasn't over. Not by a long shot. They had escaped, but only barely. And Lil Ron would come after them, harder than ever.

They drove in silence, the tension thick in the air. Erica felt a mix of relief and terror, her hands still trembling from the encounter. She looked at Quan, his face set in a grim expression. They had made it out, but they weren't safe. Not yet.

"Where do we go now?" Erica asked, her voice barely a whisper.

Quan gripped the steering wheel, his knuckles white. "We keep moving. We find a place to lay low, regroup. We can't stop now."

Erica nodded, her mind racing. They had a long road ahead, filled with dangers and uncertainty. But they were together, and that was all that mattered. She reached over and squeezed Quan's hand, a silent promise passing between them. They would make it. They had to.

As the lights faded into the distance, Erica felt a sense of resolve. The fight wasn't over, but they were still in the game. And as long as they had each other, they would find a way to survive. The night was dark, filled with shadows and threats, but Erica refused to let fear control her. They would keep running, keep fighting, until they were truly free.

Lil Ron had underestimated her, underestimated them. And Erica was determined to prove him wrong. The escape had failed, but they weren't defeated. Not yet. They would regroup, find a new plan, and this time, they wouldn't stop until they were safe. The road ahead was uncertain, but Erica was ready to face it head-on.

Chapter 12: The Tension Mounts

The dim light from the motel's flickering sign barely penetrated the grimy window of their room. Erica sat on the edge of the bed, her body tense and alert. The room smelled of stale smoke and mildew, a stark contrast to the life she had once known. But she couldn't think about that now. The failed escape had left her and Quan in a state of constant fear, a raw, gnawing tension that never seemed to let up.

Quan stood by the window, peering through the thin curtains. His eyes scanned the parking lot, searching for any sign of trouble. It had been days since they narrowly escaped Lil Ron's clutches, and the anxiety was wearing on them both. They had been moving from one seedy motel to another, never staying in one place for too long. The constant shifting was draining, but it was necessary. Lil Ron was relentless, and they knew he wouldn't stop until he had Erica back under his control.

Erica couldn't shake the feeling of being watched. Every time she stepped outside, she felt eyes on her, an invisible presence that terrified her. Lil Ron had a network of informants, people who owed him favors, and she knew he would use every resource at his disposal to find them. The thought of being captured, of being dragged back into that life, made her stomach churn.

"We can't keep doin' this," Quan muttered, his voice low and strained. He turned away from the window, his face lined with worry. "We gotta come up with a new plan. This ain't workin.'"

Erica nodded, her fingers nervously picking at the frayed edges of the bedspread. "I know. But what can we do? He's got people everywhere. It feels like we're runnin' in circles."

Quan sat down next to her, his hand reaching out to squeeze hers. "We'll figure it out. We just gotta stay one step ahead."

Erica looked at him, her heart aching. She knew he was trying to stay strong for her, but she could see the exhaustion in his eyes. They were both running on empty, fueled by adrenaline and fear. She wanted to believe they could escape, that they could start over. But the reality of their situation felt like a noose tightening around their necks.

As the days passed, the tension only grew. Lil Ron's presence loomed over them, a constant shadow. Erica could feel the walls closing in, the pressure mounting. Every sound, every movement outside their room felt like a threat. She knew they couldn't keep living like this, constantly on the run. They needed a way out, a plan that would finally free them from Lil Ron's grasp.

One evening, as they sat in the dimly lit room, Quan pulled out a burner phone they had been using to stay off the grid. He dialed a number and waited, his expression tense. After a few rings, someone picked up on the other end.

"It's me," Quan said, his voice hushed. "We need help. It's gettin' too dangerous. Can you get us out?"

Erica watched him anxiously, her heart pounding. She couldn't hear the person on the other end, but she saw the way Quan's shoulders relaxed slightly, a sign that they might have a chance.

Quan hung up the phone and turned to her, his expression serious. "I talked to a guy I know. He can get us outta here, but it's gonna cost. We gotta meet him tomorrow night, out in the old industrial district. It's risky, but it's our best shot."

Erica felt a surge of hope, a flicker of light in the darkness. But she also felt a wave of fear. The industrial district was a dangerous place, filled with abandoned buildings and hidden dangers. It was the kind of place Lil Ron would expect them to go, and that made it all the more dangerous.

"Are you sure about this?" she asked, her voice barely above a whisper. "What if it's a trap?"

Quan shook his head, his jaw clenched. "I trust this guy. He ain't got no love for Ron. But we gotta be careful. We can't let our guard down, not for a second."

The next day felt like an eternity. Erica and Quan stayed in the motel room, laying low and preparing for their next move. Every sound outside felt amplified, every knock on the door a potential threat. They packed what little they had, ready to leave at a moment's notice. The anticipation was suffocating, the fear of the unknown a constant presence.

As night fell, they slipped out of the motel, keeping to the shadows. They drove in silence, the tension palpable. The industrial district loomed ahead, a dark, foreboding landscape of crumbling buildings and empty streets. It was the perfect place for an ambush, and Erica's nerves were on edge.

They parked the car in an alley and made their way on foot, sticking to the shadows. The air was thick with tension, every sound magnified in the stillness. Erica felt her heart racing, her palms sweaty. They reached the rendezvous point, an old, abandoned warehouse. The place was eerily quiet, the only sound the distant hum of the city.

Quan checked his watch, his eyes scanning the area. "He should be here any minute."

Erica nodded, her eyes darting around nervously. She couldn't shake the feeling that they were being watched. Her mind raced with worst-case scenarios, her fear threatening to overwhelm her.

Just as she was about to say something, a car pulled up, its headlights cutting through the darkness. Erica tensed, her hand instinctively reaching for Quan's. The car door opened, and a man stepped out. He was tall, bald and husky, his face shadowed in the dim light. Erica felt a knot form in her stomach, her instincts screaming at her to run.

"Relax," Quan whispered, sensing her fear. "That's him."

The man approached, his hands in his pockets. He glanced around, his eyes sharp and alert. "You Quan?" he asked, his voice low and gravelly.

Quan nodded, his expression guarded. "Yeah. You got what we need?"

The man nodded, pulling out a small envelope. "Everything's in here. Cash, a new car. It's all set up. You leave tonight, you disappear."

Erica felt a surge of hope, her heart pounding in her chest. This was it, their chance to escape. But just as she reached for the envelope, the sound of tires screeching broke the silence. Her blood ran cold as a familiar black SUV came barreling into view, its headlights blinding.

"It's a trap!" Erica screamed, grabbing Quan's arm.

The man cursed, shoving the envelope into Quan's hands. "Go! Get outta here!"

Chaos erupted as Lil Ron's goons poured out of the SUV, guns drawn. Quan pulled Erica behind him, firing off a shot as they sprinted towards the warehouse. Bullets whizzed past them, the sound of gunfire echoing in the night. Erica's heart raced, adrenaline pumping through her veins.

They burst through the warehouse door, the darkness swallowing them whole. Quan grabbed her hand, pulling her through the maze of old machinery and debris. The sounds of pursuit grew closer, the clatter of footsteps and shouts echoing through the empty space.

They stumbled through the dark, their breaths ragged. Erica felt a surge of desperation, her mind racing. They couldn't stop, couldn't let Lil Ron catch them.

As they reached the back of the warehouse, they found an old, rusted door. Quan shoved it open, and they stumbled into the night. The cold air hit them like a slap, the darkness a welcome cover. They sprinted towards the car waiting for them, the engine already running.

They jumped in, Quan slamming the door shut. He floored the gas, the car lurching forward. Erica looked back, her breath catching in her throat. Lil Ron and his goons were right behind them, their headlights a menacing glow in the distance.

As they sped through the night, Erica felt a mix of fear and determination. They had escaped, but only barely. Lil Ron was relentless, and she knew he wouldn't stop.

The road stretched out before them, a dark, uncertain path. But Erica was ready to face it, ready to fight for her future. The tension was mounting, the danger ever-present. But as long as they had each other, they could survive. They had to.

The night was far from over, and the battle had only just begun.

Chapter 13: The Last Stand

The streets was a battlefield, filled with echoes of gunfire and shouts. Erica's breath came in ragged gasps as she was shaken and scared. The gritty, urban reality of their situation was stark and unforgiving, and they were running out of time.

Lil Ron's voice rang out, dripping with malice and a twisted sense of ownership. "You thought you could run, huh? Thought you could get away from me?" His footsteps echoed ominously as he prowled through the debris-strewn space, searching for his prey. "I own you, Erica! Ain't nowhere you can hide!"

The car roared through the deserted streets, the city's skyline a distant glow. Erica glanced at Quan, his face contorted in pain. He pushed the gas pedal harder, her heart pounding. They were running out of time, out of options.

As they rounded a corner, Erica spotted a small, nondescript building tucked away in a dark alley. It looked like the kind of place they were looking for, a haven for those who lived on the fringes of society. What she noticed next was heartbreaking. Quan had been hit! She demanded Quan pull over.

She turned to Quan, her eyes filled with tears. "Stay with me, Quan. We're almost there."

He nodded weakly, his eyes full of pain. "I'm with you, baby. I'm with you." His voice was barely a whisper, but it gave Erica the strength she needed.

She jumped out of the car, running to the door and pounding on it. "Help! We need help!" she shouted, her voice breaking.

A moment later, the door creaked open, revealing a man in a lab coat. He looked at Erica, then at Quan slumped in the car, and nodded. "Bring him in."

Erica rushed back to the car, helping Quan out. He groaned in pain, leaning heavily on her as they stumbled inside. The man led them down a narrow hallway, the smell of antiseptic and old smoke filling the air. They entered a small, dimly lit room filled with medical equipment that looked like it had seen better days.

The man gestured to a worn-out gurney. "Lay him down. I'll take care of him."

Erica did as she was told, her heart racing. She watched as the man set to work, checking Quan's wounds and preparing to stitch him up. She felt a mix of fear and hope, the weight of everything pressing down on her. This was their last stand, their final chance to escape Lil Ron's grasp.

As the man worked, Erica stood by Quan's side, holding his hand. She looked into his eyes, seeing the pain and exhaustion there. But she also saw something else—determination, resilience, love. They had made it this far, and they would keep fighting. No matter what.

The night stretched on, filled with tension and uncertainty. Erica knew they weren't safe yet, that Lil Ron would never stop looking for them. They had made their stand, and they were still standing. The road ahead was uncertain, filled with danger and unknowns.

As the man finished stitching up Quan, he looked at Erica and nodded. "He'll be okay. But you need to keep moving. Not sure what yall got goin on but I don't want that shit here."

Erica nodded, her eyes filled with determination. "Thank you"

Chapter 14: The Aftermath

The past few days had been a blur of fear and violence, each moment bleeding into the next. Erica couldn't shake the image of Quan lying in the warehouse, bleeding and vulnerable. It was her fault. She had brought him into this mess, into a world of danger and chaos. She had dragged him into her dark, twisted reality, and now he was paying the price.

Erica's mind was a whirlwind of emotions. She loved Quan more than she had ever loved anyone, but that love felt like a curse. She was a magnet for trouble, a ticking time bomb. Lil Ron wasn't going to stop. He would come after them again, and next time, they might not be so lucky. The thought of Quan getting hurt again, or worse, because of her, was unbearable.

As Quan stirred, his eyes fluttering open, Erica forced a smile. "Hey, baby," she whispered, reaching out to take his hand. "How you feelin'?"

Quan winced, trying to sit up. "Like I got hit by a truck," he muttered, his voice weak but steady. He looked at Erica, his eyes filled with concern. "You okay?"

Erica nodded, though she felt anything but okay. She squeezed his hand, trying to hold back her tears. "Yeah, I'm fine. Just... worried 'bout you."

Quan gave her a tired smile, his eyes softening. "I'm aight. Just need some rest." He looked around, his expression darkening. "We gotta keep movin', though. We ain't safe."

Erica felt a lump form in her throat. She knew he was right. They couldn't stay in one place for too long, not with Lil Ron still out there. But the thought of leaving, of running again, felt like a death sentence. She couldn't keep putting Quan in danger. She couldn't be the reason he got hurt.

For the next few days, they stayed in a shabby motel in a small town, lying low. Quan's recovery was slow, each day a struggle against pain and fatigue. Erica barely left his side, haunted by the guilt of dragging him into her chaotic world. She couldn't shake the feeling that she was a curse, that anyone who got close to her was doomed.

As Quan slept, Erica sat by the window, staring out at the darkened street. The city was quiet, the night air thick with the smell of rain. She thought about her life, the choices she had made. She had always been a survivor, doing whatever it took to get by. But now, that survival instinct felt like a curse. She had brought nothing but pain and suffering to the people she loved.

One night, as she watched the rain drizzle down the window, Erica made a decision. It was the hardest choice she had ever made, but she knew it was the right one. She couldn't stay with Quan, couldn't keep putting him in danger. He deserved better, a life free from the chaos and violence that followed her. She had to leave, for his sake.

The next morning, Erica packed her things in silence. Her heart felt heavy, each movement a painful reminder of what she was about to do. She glanced at Quan, still sleeping, his face relaxed for the first time in days. She walked over to him, her eyes brimming with tears.

She leaned down, pressing a gentle kiss to his forehead. "I'm sorry," she whispered, her voice breaking. "I'm so sorry." She straightened, wiping her tears away. She had to be strong, had to do this for him.

Erica left the motel, her heart pounding in her chest. The city was waking up, the streets slowly coming to life. She walked through the rain-soaked streets, her mind a whirlwind of emotions. She knew she was doing the right thing, but it felt like her heart was being ripped out of her chest. She loved Quan, more than anything, but she couldn't be the reason he got hurt.

She found a small, dingy motel that was a few miles out and checked in under a fake name. The room was tiny, the bed lumpy and uncomfortable. But it didn't matter. She wasn't planning on staying long. She just needed a place to think, to figure out her next move.

Erica sat on the edge of the bed, staring at the worn-out carpet. Her mind was a chaotic mess of guilt, fear, and heartbreak. She had left Quan without a word, without an explanation. She had abandoned him, and the thought tore her apart. But she knew it was for the best. He was safer without her, free from the danger that seemed to follow her everywhere.

As the hours passed, Erica felt a sense of emptiness settle in her chest. She had spent so long running, so long fighting to survive. But now, she felt lost, adrift in a sea of uncertainty. She didn't know where to go, what to do. All she knew was that she couldn't go back to her old life. She couldn't go back to Lil Ron, couldn't go back to being a pawn in his twisted game.

That night, Erica lay in the motel bed, staring at the ceiling. The room was silent, the only sound the occasional drip of water from a leaky faucet. She felt alone, more alone than she had ever felt in her life. She had left behind the one person who had ever truly cared for her, all in the name of protecting him. But now, she was left with nothing but the crushing weight of her guilt and regret.

As she lay there, Erica thought about the future. She knew what she had to do. And the thought of leaving everything behind, of starting over from scratch, felt like a monumental task.

The next morning, Erica packed her things and checked out of the motel. She started the day tryna figure out her next move, her mind racing with thoughts of Quan. She wondered how he was doing, if he was angry at her for leaving. But she couldn't dwell on that now. She had to stay focused, had to keep moving.

As she walked, Erica felt a strange sense of clarity. She knew what she had to do. She had to go back. It was the only way to protect Quan, the only way to keep him safe. She would miss him, miss their time together, but it was a sacrifice she had to make.

Erica stopped at a payphone and dialed a number she knew by heart. The line rang twice before a familiar voice answered. "Yeah?"

"It's me," Erica said, her voice steady. "Hey."

There was a pause on the other end of the line. "Hey?"

"I'm done running," Erica replied, her heart pounding. "For good."

The voice on the other end was silent for a moment. Then, with a sigh, the person spoke. "You know what you're sayin', right? This ain't no game."

"I know," Erica said, her voice firm.

There was another pause. "Aight. Meet me at the usual spot. We can work somethin' out."

Erica hung up the phone, her heart racing. She knew this was it, the point of no return. She was about to return to the very life she wanted to escape, everything she wanted to leave behind. But she had to do it, for Quan, for herself. It was the only way.

As she walked away from the payphone, Erica felt a sense of resolve. She was leaving Quan, but it was for the best. She had to believe that. She had to believe that she was doing the right thing.

Chapter 15: Lil Ron's Ultimatum

The city was bathed in a murky twilight, the kind of dusk that seemed to swallow the streets whole. Erica's heart pounded in her chest as she made her way through the narrow alleys, the weight of her decision pressing down on her. The plan was simple yet dangerous: return to Lil Ron, pretend to comply, and keep Quan safe. She knew it was a gamble, but it was the only way to protect the man she loved.

The building where Lil Ron conducted his business loomed ahead, a grim reminder of the life she had tried to escape. The place was a fortress, guarded by his loyal henchmen, men who would do anything for a cut of the dirty money that flowed through Ron's empire. As Erica approached the entrance, she felt the familiar sting of fear. She knew she was walking into the lion's den, but she had no choice. Quan's life depended on it.

The door creaked open, revealing one of Lil Ron's goons. He eyed Erica with a mix of suspicion and disdain, his hand resting on the gun holstered at his side. "What you doin' here?" he sneered, his voice rough.

Erica forced herself to remain calm, her expression blank. "I need to see Ron," she said, her voice steady. "I ain't here to cause trouble. Just need to talk."

The goon grunted, looking her up and down. After a moment, he stepped aside, gesturing for her to enter. "He's in his office. You know the way."

Erica nodded, stepping past him. The hallway was dimly lit, the air thick with the scent of cigarette smoke and stale beer. Her footsteps echoed softly as she made her way to the office door, each step a reminder of the danger she was putting herself in. She paused for a moment, taking a deep breath before knocking.

"Come in," came Lil Ron's voice from inside, cold and commanding.

Erica pushed the door open, her heart racing. Lil Ron sat behind his desk, a cigarette dangling from his lips. His eyes were sharp, calculating, as he looked up at her. The room was dim, the only light coming from a flickering desk lamp. The walls were lined with photographs and newspaper clippings, trophies of his power and influence.

"Well, well, well," Ron drawled, leaning back in his chair. "Look who decided to come back. You got some nerve showin' your face around here after the stunt you pulled."

Erica swallowed hard, forcing herself to meet his gaze. "I ain't got nowhere else to go," she said, her voice low. "You win, Ron. I'll do whatever you want. Just leave Quan out of it."

Lil Ron raised an eyebrow, a smirk playing on his lips. "Oh, so now you care about what happens to that punk-ass nigga? Funny, 'cause last I checked, you was tryin' to run off with him."

Erica clenched her fists, fighting the urge to lash out. She had to play this right, had to make him believe she was compliant. "I messed up," she admitted, her voice barely above a whisper. "But I'm here now, ain't I? I'm ready to do whatever you say."

Lil Ron studied her for a moment, his eyes cold and calculating. Then he leaned forward, flicking the ash from his cigarette onto the floor. "You think you can just waltz back in here and everything's gonna be cool? Nah, bitch, it don't work like that. You gotta earn your place back."

Erica felt a chill run down her spine. She knew this wasn't going to be easy, but the reality of the situation was hitting her hard. "What do you want me to do?" she asked, her voice trembling slightly.

Lil Ron leaned back in his chair, taking a long drag from his cigarette. "First things first, you gonna cut all ties with that nigga Quan. I don't want you seein' him, talkin' to him, nothin'. You belong to me, and you gonna act like it."

Erica's heart sank. She had expected this, but hearing it out loud made it all the more real. "Okay," she said, nodding. "I won't see him. Just... don't hurt him."

Ron chuckled, a low, menacing sound. "Oh, I ain't gonna hurt him. Not unless you give me a reason to. You fuck up, and I'll make sure he pays the price. You understand?"

Erica nodded, her stomach twisting with fear and anger. She hated the power Ron had over her, hated the way he controlled her life. But she had to play along, had to keep him from suspecting anything. "I understand," she said, her voice hollow.

Ron stubbed out his cigarette, leaning forward with a cruel smile. "Good. Now, you gonna go back to work. Start makin' me some money again. And don't think I ain't gonna be watchin' you. I got eyes everywhere, girl. You step outta line, and it's over for you and Quan."

Erica nodded again, feeling a sense of resignation settle over her. She had known this would be hard, but the reality was even worse than she had imagined. She was back in the life she had fought so hard to escape, under the control of a man who saw her as nothing more than a possession.

As she left Ron's office, Erica felt a heavy weight on her shoulders. The hallway seemed darker, the air thicker. She knew she had to be careful, had to play the part of the obedient girl if she wanted to keep Quan safe. But every step she took felt like a betrayal, a step further away from the life she wanted and deeper into the darkness she had tried to leave behind.

The next few days were a blur of surveillance and control. Lil Ron tightened his grip on Erica, monitoring her every move. He had her followed, her phone tapped, making sure she stayed in line. Every time she went out, one of his men was there, watching her, reminding her of the power he held over her life. She felt like a prisoner, trapped in a life she no longer wanted.

Erica went through the motions, returning to the streets, doing what Ron expected of her. She felt numb, disconnected from the world around her. The gritty reality of the street life mentality was her constant companion, a reminder of the consequences of defying Ron. She saw the fear in the eyes of the girls she worked with, the hopelessness that came with being trapped in this life.

But Erica knew she couldn't give up. She had to find a way out, a way to protect Quan and herself. She couldn't let Ron win, couldn't let him control her forever. She was determined to find a way to escape, to break free from the chains that bound her.

Chapter 16: The Undercover Plot

On this night the air was heavy with tension as Erica sat in a dimly lit bar, her mind racing. The place was a far cry from the glamorous clubs Lil Ron frequented and sent her to meet high end clientele . This bar was gritty and worn, filled with people looking for a stiff drink to wash away their troubles. Erica kept her head low, her hoodie pulled tight around her face, trying to blend in. She was here for a reason, and it wasn't for the watered-down whiskey.

Across from her sat Jax, an old friend from the neighborhood who had managed to stay out of trouble, at least most of the time. Jax had always been a hustler, but he had a good heart. He knew the streets better than anyone, and Erica trusted him. She had reached out to him, desperate for a way out, and he had suggested something that had been gnawing at her ever since.

"You gotta think 'bout workin' with the cops," Jax said, his voice low and serious. He leaned forward, his eyes scanning the bar for any sign of trouble. "I know it ain't what you wanna hear, but it's the only way to bring Ron down. You go undercover, get the evidence they need, and they take his ass down."

Erica felt her stomach twist at the thought. The idea of working with the police made her skin crawl. In the world she lived in, cops were the enemy, the ones who could ruin your life with a single arrest. She had spent years avoiding them, staying out of their way. But now, Jax was suggesting she turn to them for help, to betray everything she had known.

"I dunno, Jax," Erica muttered, taking a sip of her drink. The liquid burned her throat, a harsh reminder of the reality she was trying to escape. "You know what happens to people who snitch. Ron finds out, and I'm dead. Quan's dead. Hell, anyone who ever knew me is dead."

Jax sighed, rubbing a hand over his shaved head. "I get it, girl. I do. But you gotta think long-term. Ron's got his claws in deep, and he ain't lettin' go. You keep runnin', and he keeps comin'. This is the only way to end it, for real."

Erica looked down at her drink, her mind racing. She had been running for so long, fighting to survive. But the thought of going against Ron, of turning him over to the cops, felt like stepping into a lion's den. It wasn't just about her own safety; it was about the people she cared about. She couldn't bear the thought of putting them at risk, of bringing the wrath of Lil Ron down on them.

"I ain't no snitch," Erica said, her voice barely above a whisper. She felt a lump in her throat, a mixture of fear and guilt. "But I can't keep doin' this. I can't keep lookin' over my shoulder, waitin' for Ron to show up."

Jax nodded, his expression sympathetic. "I know it ain't easy, E. But you gotta think 'bout your future, 'bout gettin' outta this life. The cops, they can protect you. Witness protection, new identity, the whole deal. You just gotta get them what they need."

Erica felt cold chills. The idea of leaving everything behind, starting over with a new name, a new life, was both terrifying and tempting. But it wasn't just about her. She thought about Quan, about the life they wanted to build together. She couldn't leave him behind, couldn't abandon him. But staying meant constant danger, a life on the run.

As the night wore on, Erica wrestled with her thoughts. She knew Jax was right, that working with the cops might be the only way to finally break free from Lil Ron's grip. But the risks were enormous. She would be putting herself in the crosshairs, exposing herself to the dangers of the criminal underworld. And if anything went wrong, if Ron found out, it would be a death sentence.

The bar was starting to empty out, the buzz of conversation dwindling. Erica looked at Jax, her eyes filled with uncertainty. "How do I even start?" she asked, her voice trembling. "How do I even go to the cops and say, 'Hey, I wanna bring down one of the biggest players in the city'?"

Jax leaned back in his chair, his eyes thoughtful. "You start by findin' someone you can trust, someone who ain't on Ron's payroll. You gotta be careful, though. This ain't somethin' you can just jump into. You make one wrong move, and it's all over."

Erica nodded, her mind racing with possibilities. She knew she had to be smart, had to plan every step carefully. The stakes were too high to make a mistake. But the more she thought about it, the more she realized that this might be her only way out. She couldn't keep living in fear, couldn't keep running from Lil Ron. She had to take a stand, to fight back.

As the last call was announced and the bar began to close, Erica felt a sense of calmness. She knew what she had to do, even if it scared her. She had to take the risk, had to find a way to bring Lil Ron to justice. It was the only way to protect herself and the people she loved.

She stood up, her legs feeling shaky. "Thanks, Jax," she said, her voice steady. "I gotta think 'bout this, but... I think you're right."

Jax nodded, his expression serious. "Just be careful, E. You go down this road, and there ain't no turnin' back. But if anyone can do it, it's you."

Erica forced a smile, feeling a surge of determination. She knew this was dangerous, knew that she was stepping into uncharted territory. But she couldn't keep living in fear, couldn't keep letting Lil Ron control her life. She had to take a stand, had to fight for her freedom.

As she left the bar and stepped into the cool night air, Erica felt a sense of purpose. The city stretched out before her, a sprawling labyrinth of danger and possibility. She knew the road ahead would be tough, filled with heavy risks. But she was ready to do whatever it took to bring Lil Ron down.

The idea of working with the police still made her uneasy, but she knew it was the only way. She had to gather evidence, had to build a case strong enough to put Ron away for good. It wouldn't be easy, and it would be dangerous. But Erica was ready. She had spent too long living in the shadows, hiding from the dangers of her past. It was time to step into the light, to take control of her destiny.

Chapter 17: The Betrayal

The room was dimly lit, filled with the acrid smell of cigarette smoke and cheap air freshener. Erica sat at the small, wobbly table, her hands clasped tightly in her lap. Across from her sat Detective Harris, a grizzled veteran of the force with a face that looked like it had seen one too many hard days. He had been the only cop Jax trusted, a rare breed who wasn't on the take and had a reputation for getting things done.

"You sure about this, Erica?" Harris asked, his voice low and gravelly. He leaned back in his chair, scrutinizing her with a keen eye. "Once we go through with this, there ain't no turnin' back."

Erica took a deep breath, her mind racing with the gravity of her decision. She had spent days agonizing over it, weighing the risks and the consequences. But in the end, she knew she had to do it. Lil Ron had terrorized her and countless others for too long. This was her chance to finally bring him down, to end the nightmare once and for all.

"I'm sure," she said, her voice steady despite the turmoil inside her. "But you gotta promise me, Quan stays outta this. He ain't done nothin' wrong."

Harris nodded, his expression serious. "We'll do what we can. But once the shit hits the fan, it's gonna be messy. You just make sure you get the evidence we need."

Erica nodded, feeling a knot tighten in her stomach. The plan was simple but dangerous: she would gather incriminating evidence against Lil Ron, enough to put him away for a long time. The cops would swoop in and bust him, ending his reign of terror. It sounded straightforward, but Erica knew better. Nothing ever went according to plan, especially in the streets.

As she left the meeting, Erica felt a mix of fear and resolve. She had made her choice, and now she had to see it through. But the closer she got to the day of the bust, the more she felt the weight of her decision.

She knew Ron had eyes everywhere, and if he even got a whiff of what she was planning, it would be over for her and anyone she cared about.

The days passed in a blur of tension and paranoia. Erica went back to her routine, playing the role of the loyal girl, pretending to be compliant while secretly gathering evidence. She wore a wire during her meetings with Ron, capturing every incriminating word. It was nerve-wracking, knowing that one slip-up could blow her cover. But she kept her cool, doing her best to stay under the radar.

Lil Ron seemed oblivious, still treating her like his possession, barking orders and expecting obedience. But there was an undercurrent of suspicion in his eyes, a wariness that made Erica's skin crawl. She knew he was dangerous, knew that he wouldn't hesitate to kill her if he found out what she was up to. But she had to keep going, had to see this through.

The night of the bust finally arrived. The plan was set, the police ready to move in as soon as Erica gave the signal. She sat in the back room of one of Ron's clubs, her heart pounding in her chest. The room was filled with the sounds of loud music and the chatter of people, but all Erica could focus on was the small wire taped to her chest. She felt like she was walking on a tightrope, every step precarious and fraught with danger.

Ron was in a good mood, celebrating a new deal that would bring in a lot of cash. He lounged on a plush sofa, surrounded by his crew, laughing and boasting about his latest exploits. Erica sat beside him, forcing herself to smile, to play along. But inside, she was a bundle of nerves, her mind racing with thoughts of what was about to happen.

As the night wore on, Ron excused himself to take a call. Erica watched him go, her heart in her throat. This was it. She knew the cops were waiting, listening to everything through the wire. She just had to get Ron to say the right words, to incriminate himself beyond a shadow of a doubt.

Ron returned, his expression dark. He glanced around the room, his eyes narrowing. Erica felt a chill run down her spine. Something was wrong. She could see it in his face, the way his jaw tightened, the way he avoided her gaze.

He walked over to her, his face a mask of anger. "We need to talk," he said, grabbing her arm and pulling her towards the back office. Erica's heart raced, fear coursing through her veins. She followed him, trying to keep her composure, but inside she was terrified.

Once they were inside the office, Ron slammed the door shut and turned to her, his eyes blazing with fury. "You think I'm stupid, bitch?" he spat, his voice low and menacing. "You think I don't know what you been up to?"

Erica felt her blood run cold. She forced herself to play dumb, to act confused. "What are you talkin' 'bout, Ron? I ain't done nothin.'"

Ron sneered, grabbing her by the shoulders and shaking her. "Don't play games with me, Erica! I know you been workin' with the cops. I got people everywhere, remember? You really thought you could pull this shit off and get away with it?"

Erica's mind raced, panic setting in. How had he found out? Had someone tipped him off? She felt the wire under her shirt, a cold reminder of the danger she was in. She had to keep him talking, had to get him to say something incriminating.

"I don't know what you're talkin' 'bout, Ron," she said, trying to keep her voice steady. "You got it all wrong."

Ron laughed, a cold, bitter sound. "Oh, I got it wrong, huh? Then explain this." He pulled out a small recorder from his pocket and hit play. Erica's heart sank as she heard her own voice, talking to Detective Harris, discussing the plan. She felt like the ground had opened up beneath her, swallowing her whole.

"You're done, Erica," Ron said, his voice cold and deadly. "You think you can fuck with me and get away with it? I will fucking kill you bitch!"

Erica's mind raced, searching for a way out. She had to think fast, had to find a way to salvage the situation. But before she could say anything, the door burst open and the room was flooded with police officers. Guns drawn, they stormed in, shouting orders and demanding everyone to get on the ground.

Ron cursed, reaching for his gun, but it was too late. The cops were on him in an instant, pinning him to the ground. Erica felt a strange mix of relief and fear wash over her. The bust had gone down, but not the way she had planned. She watched as the officers cuffed Ron, his face twisted in rage and betrayal.

As the dust settled, Detective Harris walked over to Erica, his expression grim. "You okay?" he asked, his voice low.

Erica nodded, her heart still pounding. "Yeah, I think so."

Harris sighed, glancing at Ron. "We got him. But it was close. Too close."

Erica felt a lump in her throat. She had known the risks but seeing it all play out had been terrifying. She looked at Ron, now being dragged away in cuffs, and felt a strange sense of finality. But was it over? Was the nightmare finally over?

But as she stood there, watching the chaos around her, Erica couldn't shake the feeling of unease. She had betrayed Ron, but in doing so, she had also betrayed a part of herself. She had crossed a line, and there was no going back. The streets had their own code, their own rules, and she had broken them.

As the police escorted her out of the building, Erica felt a sense of emptiness settle over her. She had done what she had to do, but it had come at a cost. The road ahead was uncertain, filled with unknowns. But one thing was clear: she could never go back to the life she had known. She was a different person now, and the streets would never forget.

Chapter 18: The Deadly Night

The city streets were eerily quiet as the night descended, a thick fog rolling in from the bay, wrapping the buildings in a ghostly shroud. Erica felt the chill in the air as she walked alongside Quan, her mind heavy with the weight of recent events. Lil Ron had been arrested, but the news of him bonding out had spread like wildfire. Erica knew that Ron wouldn't let this slide, and the streets were buzzing with the anticipation of retaliation. She felt the familiar tightness in her chest, a mixture of fear and resignation.

They had found temporary refuge in an old friend's apartment, a rundown building on the edge of the city. It wasn't much, but it was safe, for now. As they reached the apartment, Erica glanced at Quan, his face a mask of worry. He had insisted on sticking by her side, despite the danger. She admired his loyalty but feared for his safety. She knew Ron would come for her, and she couldn't bear the thought of Quan getting caught in the crossfire.

Inside the apartment, the tension was palpable. The place was sparse, just a worn-out couch and a small table cluttered with takeout containers. Erica and Quan settled in, trying to relax, but the unease hung heavy in the air. Erica kept glancing at the door, half expecting it to burst open at any moment. The city outside felt like a powder keg ready to explode, and they were right in the middle of it.

As the hours passed, the silence grew more oppressive. Erica felt like she was living on borrowed time, each second ticking away like a countdown. She couldn't shake the feeling that something terrible was about to happen. She stood by the window, peering through the blinds at the deserted street below. The fog had thickened, making it hard to see more than a few feet ahead. It was the perfect cover for someone like Ron.

Quan joined her at the window, placing a comforting hand on her shoulder. "We gonna get through this, E," he said softly, his voice steady. "Just don't leave me again we can get thru this."

Erica nodded, though she wasn't convinced. She knew Ron too well, knew how ruthless he could be. He wouldn't stop until he got what he wanted. "I hope you're right," she muttered, her eyes scanning the foggy street. "I just got a bad feelin' 'bout tonight."

As if on cue, a car screeched to a halt outside the building. Erica's heart leaped into her throat. She could make out the silhouette of a black SUV, its headlights cutting through the fog. She knew that car. It was Ron's. Her blood ran cold as she watched the doors swing open, and shadowy figures emerged, moving quickly toward the building.

"Quan, we gotta go!" Erica hissed, grabbing his arm. Panic surged through her as she realized they were out of time. "He's here!"

Quan's eyes widened, and he grabbed the gun they had stashed under the couch. "Fuckkkkk," he muttered, his voice tight with fear. They scrambled to the back of the apartment, looking for an escape route. The fire escape was their only option, a narrow metal ladder leading down to the alley below.

Just as they reached the window, the door to the apartment burst open. Ron's voice echoed through the room, dripping with rage. "You rat ass bitch! You think you can play me like a fool?"

Erica felt a surge of adrenaline as she turned to face him. Ron stood in the doorway, a gun in his hand, flanked by two of his goons. His eyes were wild, a mix of anger and betrayal. He raised the gun, pointing it at Erica, his face contorted with fury.

"You think you can just snitch on me and walk away?" Ron snarled, his voice low and dangerous. "You got shit fucked up."

Before Erica could react, Ron pulled the trigger. The gunshot rang out, deafening in the confined space. Erica felt a sharp pain in her side, the force of the impact knocking her back. She stumbled, her vision blurring as she clutched her side. Blood seeped through her fingers, warm and sticky.

Quan shouted, firing back at Ron and his men. The room erupted into chaos, bullets flying in all directions. Erica struggled to stay on her feet, the pain searing through her body. She could hear Quan's voice, shouting her name, but it sounded distant, like it was coming from underwater.

Time seemed to slow as Erica looked up, her vision fading. She saw Ron advancing, his face twisted in a cruel smile. He raised his gun again, aiming straight at her. In that moment, Erica knew it was over. She had fought so hard, tried to escape the darkness, but it had finally caught up to her.

Another gunshot rang out, and Erica felt a sharp pain in her chest. She gasped, her breath hitching as she fell to the floor. The world around her dimmed, the sounds of the chaos fading into a distant murmur. She felt cold, her body growing numb.

As she lay there, her vision fading, Erica felt a strange sense of peace. She had done her best, had tried to find a way out. But in the end, the streets had claimed her, just like so many others. She thought of Quan, her heart aching with regret. She wished she could have told him she loved him one last time.

In the distance, she heard sirens, the wail of police cars approaching. But it was too late. The darkness was closing in, pulling her under. Erica took one last, shuddering breath, and then everything went black.

Quan's voice was the last thing she heard, a desperate cry echoing in the darkness. "Erica! No!"

As the sirens grew louder, the room was bathed in red and blue lights. Ron and his men fled, leaving behind a scene of devastation. Quan knelt beside Erica, his hands shaking as he cradled her lifeless body. Tears streamed down his face, mixing with the blood that stained the floor.

The police stormed in, guns drawn, shouting orders. But the battle was over. Lil Ron had escaped, and Erica was gone. The room was filled with the aftermath of violence, the air thick with the smell of gunpowder and blood.

As the medics arrived and tried to pull Quan away, he clung to Erica, refusing to let go. His voice was choked with grief, a raw, guttural sound. "She didn't deserve this," he whispered, his voice breaking. "She didn't deserve any of this."

The medics finally pried him away, and Quan watched helplessly as they covered Erica's body with a sheet. The room was filled with the flashing lights of the police cars, the chaos of the scene overwhelming. But all Quan could focus on was the cold, lifeless form on the floor, the woman he loved taken from him in an instant.

As the night wore on and the city slowly woke up to the news of the violence, Quan stood alone, his heart shattered. He knew he had lost more than just Erica. He had lost the hope of a better life, the dream of escaping the darkness. The streets had claimed another victim, leaving behind nothing but pain and sorrow.

The night was deadly, the consequences irreversible. Lil Ron had struck a final, cruel blow, leaving a scar that would never heal. And as the city moved on, another story in the cycle of violence and despair, Quan was left to pick up the pieces, to mourn the woman he had loved and lost.

In the end, the streets had won, leaving behind a trail of destruction and heartbreak. Erica's struggle for a better life had ended in tragedy, a cruel reminder of the harsh realities of the world they lived in. The darkness had claimed her, and there was no escaping its grasp.

Chapter 19: The Fallout

The morning after the deadly night was thick with a somber haze, the city's usual hum of life muted by the weight of what had transpired. The streets were quiet, whispers of the night's violence spreading like wildfire through the cracks and alleys. Lil Ron had been arrested, but the streets buzzed with a mixture of relief and dread. The cost had been high, and the echoes of gunfire still rang in the minds of those who had been close enough to hear.

Quan sat on the steps of an old tenement building, his eyes vacant, staring at the ground. The world around him seemed distant, a blur of noise and movement that didn't quite reach him. Erica was gone. The reality of it was a crushing weight on his chest, a pain so deep it felt like he couldn't breathe. The love of his life, the woman he had fought so hard to protect, was gone. And all that was left was an empty space where she used to be.

He could still see her face, still hear her laugh. But now it was all tainted by the memory of her lying on the floor, lifeless. He had replayed the scene over and over in his head, trying to find some way it could have ended differently. But there was no escaping the truth. Erica was gone, and Lil Ron had made sure of that.

As Quan sat there, lost in his grief, the city around him buzzed with gossip and speculation. People whispered about what had happened, each story more embellished than the last. In the streets, at the barbershops, in the corner stores, everyone had something to say. And much of it wasn't kind.

"She had it comin', messin' with a nigga like Ron," one woman said, shaking her head as she stood outside a bodega. "You don't play with fire and expect not to get burned."

"Yeah, but she was tryin' to get out," another man argued, his voice low. "She was workin' with the cops, tryna bring him down. She ain't deserve to die like that."

"But she knew what she was doin,'" someone else chimed in, their voice harsh. "You can't snitch and not expect repercussions. She brought all this on herself."

The words stung, a cruel reminder of the harsh realities of their world. In the ghetto, loyalty was everything, and snitches were despised. Erica's actions had been brave, but to many, they were also seen as a betrayal. The streets had their own code, and breaking it came with a heavy price. Quan knew that all too well.

As the day wore on, the police presence in the neighborhood was thick. The flashing lights of squad cars were a stark reminder of the chaos that had unfolded. Lil Ron had been caught, dragged away in cuffs, but not before wreaking havoc. The cops had him on enough charges to put him away for a long time, but the damage had already been done.

Quan couldn't shake the feeling of guilt that gnawed at him. He felt like he had failed Erica, like he hadn't done enough to protect her. The thought of her final moments haunted him, the look in her eyes as she realized it was over. He wished he could turn back time, change the course of events, but he knew it was futile. Erica was gone, and all he could do was pick up the pieces of his shattered life.

The streets were ruthless, and the gossip only fueled the fire. Erica's name was dragged through the mud, her memory tainted by rumors and half-truths. People whispered about her involvement with the cops, about how she had tried to bring Lil Ron down. They blamed her for the violence, for the bloodshed. It was easier to point fingers than to acknowledge the complex reality of the situation.

Quan found himself caught in the crossfire of these rumors. People looked at him with a mix of pity and disdain, as if he were somehow responsible for what had happened. He felt isolated, cut off from the world he had once known. His friends were wary, unsure of how to approach him. The weight of his loss and the stigma attached to Erica's actions left him feeling alone in his grief.

As the sun began to set, casting long shadows across the streets, Quan knew he couldn't stay here. The memories were too painful, the whispers too loud. He had to leave, to find a way to escape the suffocating grief that threatened to consume him. He stood up, his body heavy with exhaustion, and walked aimlessly through the city. The night air was cool, a stark contrast to the heat of the day.

He wandered to a small park, a place where he and Erica had often come to escape the chaos of the streets. He sat on a bench, the memories flooding back. He remembered the way she used to laugh, the way she would talk about their future, about leaving the city and starting over. Now those dreams felt like distant echoes, lost in the wake of her death.

As he sat there, Quan realized that he had to leave. The city was filled with too many ghosts, too many reminders of what he had lost. He couldn't stay here, surrounded by the memories and the pain. He needed a fresh start, a chance to heal and move forward. But leaving meant saying goodbye to Erica, to the life they had tried to build together.

The decision weighed heavily on him, but he knew it was the only way. He couldn't keep reliving the past, couldn't keep torturing himself with what-ifs and regrets. Erica was gone, and he had to find a way to live without her. It was a painful realization, but it was the truth.

Quan stood up, taking one last look at the park. He felt a pang of sadness, a deep ache in his chest. But he knew he couldn't stay. He had to move on, to find a way to live with the pain. As he walked away, the city lights flickering around him, he felt a sense of finality. The chapter was closing, and a new one was beginning.

He didn't know where he would go, or what he would do. But he knew he had to leave, to find a place where he could start over. The streets had taken so much from him, but they couldn't take his hope. He would find a way to honor Erica's memory, to live the life she had wanted for them.

As Quan disappeared into the night, the city continued to buzz with gossip and rumors. But he didn't care. He was leaving it all behind, the pain, the whispers, the stigma. He was setting out on a new path, uncertain but determined. And as he walked away, he carried Erica's memory with him, a bittersweet reminder of the love they had shared and the life they had tried to build.

Chapter 20: Reflection and Redemption

The rain fell in a steady rhythm, a melancholic soundtrack to the gray morning. Quan stood at the edge of the cemetery, his hands shoved deep into the pockets of his worn leather jacket. The fresh grave was a stark reminder of the life that had been lost, a final resting place for the woman he had loved. Erica's funeral had been a quiet affair, attended by a handful of people who had known her. As the last of the mourners drifted away, Quan remained, rooted in place, lost in his thoughts.

He stared at the simple headstone, the words etched into the stone a painful reminder of the reality he faced. "Erica Marie Thompson, Beloved Daughter and Friend." The words felt hollow, inadequate to capture the complexity of the woman she had been. Erica had been so much more than the mistakes she made or the life she had been trapped in. She had been vibrant, full of dreams and hopes, even in the darkest moments.

As the rain soaked through his clothes, Quan felt a coldness seep into his bones. He couldn't shake the image of Erica's face, the way she had smiled at him, the sound of her laughter. They had been happy, even if it had been fleeting. He had seen a future with her, a life away from the streets and the violence. But that future had been stolen from them, ripped away by the harsh realities of their world.

Quan knelt down, placing a small bouquet of wildflowers at the base of the headstone. The flowers were a meager offering, a symbol of the love he still held for her. As he knelt there, he couldn't help but reflect on their relationship, the whirlwind of emotions that had defined their time together. They had been two lost souls, clinging to each other in a world that seemed determined to tear them apart.

"Why'd it have to end like this, E?" Quan muttered, his voice barely audible over the sound of the rain. "We was supposed to get out, start over. But now you gone, and I'm still here, tryin' to make sense of it all."

The wind picked up, rustling the leaves of the nearby trees. Quan closed his eyes, letting the cold air wash over him. He thought about the life Erica had led, the choices she had made. She had been caught in the allure of the fast life, drawn to the money and the danger. But it had also been her undoing. The streets had a way of sucking people in, of offering them an escape while simultaneously trapping them in a cycle of violence and despair.

Erica's story had become a cautionary tale, a stark reminder of the dangers of the street life. Quan knew that the rumors and gossip would continue to swirl, painting Erica as a cautionary tale, a tragic figure caught in a world she couldn't escape. But he also knew there was more to her than that. She had been a fighter, someone who had tried to break free from the chains that bound her. In the end, the streets had claimed her, but they hadn't defined her.

As Quan stood, he felt a sense of clarity wash over him. He couldn't change the past, couldn't bring Erica back. But he could honor her memory, could live a life that reflected the lessons he had learned from their time together. He had been given a second chance, and he wasn't going to waste it.

He turned away from the grave, his thoughts heavy with the weight of his reflections. The city stretched out before him, a sprawling landscape of concrete and steel. It was a place filled with both danger and possibility, a place where lives could be made or broken in an instant. Quan knew he couldn't escape the city, couldn't run from the past. But he could choose how he moved forward.

As he walked through the cemetery gates, Quan thought about the allure of the fast life, the seductive pull of easy money and quick thrills. It was a world that promised so much but delivered so little. He had seen firsthand the cost of that life, the way it chewed people up and spit them out. Erica had been a victim of that world, but she had also been a beacon of hope, a reminder that even in the darkest moments, there was always a choice.

Quan knew that the road ahead wouldn't be easy. The streets were unforgiving, and the scars of his past would always be with him. But he was determined to rise above it, to find a way to live a life that honored Erica's memory. He would take the lessons he had learned and use them to build something better, something real.

In the end, Erica's story was a reminder of the harsh realities of the street life, a world where love and loyalty were tested in the most brutal ways. But it was also a story of redemption, of the possibility of change and the power of choice. And as Quan walked into the future, he carried that story with him, a beacon of hope in a world that could be so dark remembering that with every ending there is also a new beginning.

Don't miss out!

Visit the website below and you can sign up to receive emails whenever Rachael Reed publishes a new book. There's no charge and no obligation.

https://books2read.com/r/B-A-WXARB-CBJSE

BOOKS 2 READ

Connecting independent readers to independent writers.

Did you love *Can't Turn a Hoe Into a Housewife*? Then you should read *The Virgin and The Kingpin*[1] by Rachael Reed!

[2]

In the heart of Cancun, where paradise masks the gritty reality of city streets, two worlds collide. Megan Moore, a virgin and career-driven woman on a much-needed vacation with her best friend, is determined to escape her troubles back home. Enter Jerel Phillips, a suave, ruthless drug kingpin escaping his own chaos. For seven days, they share a fiery connection, exploring the depths of desire and secrets they never imagined revealing.

But paradise ain't forever. As their planes depart, they return to their chaotic lives, unable to forget the spark that ignited in Cancun. Back in the gritty, unforgiving streets, Megan and Jerel stay in touch, their bond deepening against all odds. Megan finds herself drawn into

---

1. https://books2read.com/u/3GlO8a

2. https://books2read.com/u/3GlO8a

Jerel's dark, dangerous world—a world filled with long prison sentences, baby mama drama, theft, murder, and betrayal.

As their relationship intensifies, so does the danger. Jerel's empire faces threats from rivals and the law, while Megan grapples with the reality of loving a kingpin. Secrets unravel, lies are exposed, and trust is shattered. The stakes climb higher as they navigate a world where loyalty is tested and betrayal lurks at every corner.

With their lives on the line, Megan and Jerel must fight for their love and survival. Will they conquer the treacherous streets together, or will their worlds tear them apart? One thing's for sure—what happens on vacation doesn't always stay on vacation.

Get ready for a gripping, emotional rollercoaster that delves deep into the dark underbelly of city living. This is urban fiction at its rawest, where love and loyalty are put to the ultimate test, and every page leaves you hanging on the edge, craving more. Can they escape the shadows, or will their pasts consume them? Dive into "The Virgin and the Kingpin" and find out.

Also by Rachael Reed

Codefendant
Codefendant
Once a Cheater
Once a Cheater
Passport Bro
What Happens in Prison
Preference
Sprinkle Sprinkle
Championship Bad
Street Exodus
Street Exodus
Street Royalty
Pawns of Power
SIS
Cartel Bloodline
Get Money Girls
Skip the Games
Til Death Do Us Part
Backpage Hustle
Link in Bio
The Virgin and The Kingpin
A Gangsta's Heart
Boosters
Can't Turn a Hoe Into a Housewife

www.ingramcontent.com/pod-product-compliance
Lightning Source LLC
Chambersburg PA
CBHW031210160726
47992CB00006B/2665